Praise for Cindy Procter-King

"Simply enchanting!"

— InD'tale Magazine on BEFORE
BRADY

"What a set-up for a comedy of errors! Everything that can go wrong in this scenario does go wrong, and the reader is well entertained by the comedic chaos."

— Fallen Angel Reviews on HEAD
OVER HEELS

"I really enjoyed *Borrowing Alex*. It was smart and funny without being overdone. The characters do some pretty funny things in the name of love. I am definitely looking forward to reading the next book I find by Cindy Procter-King."

— Joyfully Reviewed on BORROWING
ALEX

"I really like romantic comedy as a genre, but it takes some really good writing to make me laugh. This book made me laugh."

— Fallen Angel Reviews on
BORROWING ALEX

"*'Getting Over Brett'* is everything a romantic comedy should be!...a very funny, light and easy romance that will leave a big goofy smile on your face!"

— InD'tale Magazine on GETTING
OVER BRETT

"*Getting Over Brett* is a top-of-the-line read. It has everything you could possibly want in a modern romance. It's fun and playful at times, full of flirty banter, then deeply romantic and emotional at its heart. Somehow, it's both sweet and sexy all at the same time!"

—Julianne MacLean, USA Today
Bestselling Author

"Cindy Procter-King presents readers with a suspenseful snapshot of a romantic comedy... loaded with humor, this is a must-read."

— Night Owl Reviews on PICTURE IMPERFECT

"Procter-King has written a 'home' for all of us. Destiny Falls is the place that holds your first love, your first triumph..."

— RT Book Reviews on WHERE SHE BELONGS

Just Janie

Also by Cindy Procter-King

Steamy RomCom

Love & Other Calamities

RomCom Series

Deceiving Derek (Book 1)

Catching Claire (Book 2)

Before Brady (Book 3)

Trusting Trey (Book 5)

Love in the Pacific Northwest

Stand-alone Romantic Comedy

Head Over Heels (Book 1)

Borrowing Alex (Book 2)

Getting Over Brett (Book 3)

Contemporary Romance

Just Janie

CINDY PROCTER-KING

Blue Orchard Books

Published by Blue Orchard Books

Cover by The Killion Group

ISBN: 978-1-989113-03-5 (eBook)

ISBN: 978-1-989113-07-3 (Print)

For my dad, who followed my mom from Canada to Nashville to convince her they were meant to be together —and they are, for over 65 years and counting! Love you, Dad.

Chapter One

Sunday afternoon, July 23rd
Countdown to Tania and Trey's wedding: 6 days
(unless...)

Janie McAllister needed to get a life. No more sticking her nose into her twin brother's lack of a love life.

Oh, all right, Janie amended as she peeked at her friend Claire playing with a five-pound golden Yorkshire terrier in the sunny backyard of Mrs. Hoyt's home. Make that her brother's *former* lack of a love life. Derek didn't require her help any longer. He seemed over-the-moon with his new girlfriend, Lacey, thanks to Janie cleverly arranging the couple's first meeting.

Fingers tapping the screen of Claire's borrowed phone, Janie wiggled her behind deeper into the comfortable patio chair. Some people might say meddling in the happiness of others was a "Janie McAllister specialty." Even so, her phenomenal success rate dictated that any day now she would run out of friends to matchmake. At that point, her efforts would pirouette in a tidy one-eighty to focus on herself. But not until then.

As the fresh scent of mowed grass drifted on the Sunday afternoon breeze, Janie slipped a sidelong glance toward Claire and the frolicking dog. Good, her friend hadn't noticed Janie had swapped their phones to look up...something.

More precisely, *someone*.

Janie's ex-boyfriend, Keon Rivers.

Claire tousled Teacup's pink hairbow and laughed. "Janie, look. She's adorable."

"Yep, she's a cutie," Janie responded with a quick smile. Claire tossed Teacup's stuffed satin bone into the air. The tiny dog yipped until the floppy bone plopped onto the grass. Teacup raced in a circle for a three-second count before steely-eyeballing Claire. Another flip of the toy ensued.

Janie cheered on the pair. Moments later, Teacup scampered toward the yellow double-knockout shrub roses in a fenced corner of the yard. The Yorkie squatted.

"Whoops," Claire said, popping to her feet and pulling a compostable doggy bag out of her shorts pocket. "I might be awhile. Tania said Teacup is a little stopped up."

Tania Hoyt, the bride for a wedding occurring in six days and the first of their friends to get hitched, was Mrs. Hoyt's oldest daughter and Teacup's devoted human-mama.

"Too much information, my friend," Janie advised. On the other hand, the longer it took Teacup to accomplish her doggy business, the more phone-snooping time at Janie's disposal.

A needle of guilt prickled beneath her skin as Claire and the dog retreated to the roses. Claire had no clue that Janie had swapped their devices before the display on Claire's phone had locked. But Janie's exchange of their phones from atop the patio table couldn't be helped. A year ago, she'd obliterated *her* social media connections to Keon Rivers and wiped his contact info from her devices two weeks after he'd moved back to Canada. But Keon and Claire—and everyone else in their Rosevale and Greater Seattle friend group—had stayed in touch. As a result, Janie needed to sneak someone else's phone to monitor Keon's activities on the sly.

Nibbling a thumbnail, she accessed a site and studied his profile. A sigh slipped from her mouth. With that thick shock of coal-black hair sweeping back from his forehead, the striking liquid brown of his eyes, those full lips she recalled pressing to hers, his square jaw, and a flawless dusting of summer stubble, Keon Rivers looked as handsome and sexy as ever.

Damn him.

He hadn't posted a new photo in weeks. Were her sleuthing efforts in vain?

Her gaze drifted to a familiar picture in his feed. In the image, his arm draped around the shoulder of his latest girlfriend at a British Columbia winery across the Washington state border in Canada. The twenty-something brunette's cheerful disposition oozed from the posts tagged to Keon's profile. So annoying.

Janie scrolled.

Ah. There. Much better.

Another photo displayed Keon standing alongside his mom and dad and two younger brothers at the Hamaguchi Fruit and Garden Centre, spelled the Canadian way, ending in RE. Keon's Japanese grandparents on his mom's side immigrated to BC in the 1950s to work in the province's booming fruit-farming industry. Now, Keon headed the popular and successful garden center, which had grown from a tiny roadside stand into a bustling family enterprise.

Janie glided a fingertip over the next few photos, and her pulse kicked into overdrive at the images of her ex. The first featured Keon strapping into zip-lining gear as he prepared to soar over a dayscape of Las Vegas during the groomsmen's bachelor party trip in June. Trey, the groom for next weekend's wedding, photobombed the shot Golden-Retriever-style, gaze joyful and tongue lolling.

Next came a post of Keon in his six-foot-one, sculpted-physique glory, wet shorts clinging to his muscular thighs as he captained his paddle board on Okanagan Lake. Miles of inviting lake water, rolling hills, and clear blue skies served as his backdrop.

Janie fanned her face. Oooh-ee, her ex should have become an underwear model. The world had lost out big time on those six-pack abs and firm butt.

Then emerged a nighttime image of Keon and his brothers sitting around a blazing campfire in the Canadian woods, an open beer bottle in his hand and a bag of chips at his booted feet. No sign of the girlfriend existed in the campfire photo, the garden center picture, or the lake shot. Were they taken with the woman's phone?

Janie grunted. *Whatever*. The girlfriend's presence or absence from Keon's social feed—in his life—didn't matter one smidgen to totally-over-him Janie McAllister. She couldn't care less *who* he dated.

"Janie? Janie!"

"Crap!" Janie's head jerked upright as Claire returned to the patio, carrying Teacup. The Yorkie gripped the satin toy between tiny white teeth, and a filled-to-capacity doggy bag dangled from Claire's fingertip. Evidently, Teacup had overcome her bathroom issues.

Janie slid Claire's phone onto the pebbly glass surface of the table. Eyebrows up, Janie placed her palm over her own phone and skated the device onto her skirt-covered lap. "Yes?"

Her attempt at nonchalance did not pass muster.

Claire's forehead knotted. Her gaze cut to the table. "Is that my phone?"

"Correct. And this one's mine." Janie waved her device.

"But you were using my phone." Claire dumped Teacup onto Janie's lap. The dog dropped the stuffie and licked Janie's chin. The rough texture of the Yorkie's tongue tickled. "Why, Janie?" Claire interrogated, tossing the poop bag onto the exposed aggregate before grabbing her phone and holding the device to her chest as if protecting it from an evil sorceress. An unpleasant aroma wafted from the sack at Janie's sandaled feet. Claire shot Janie a squint. "Spying on your ex again? You can keep tabs on Keon on your own phone."

"I needed to check on something." Janie angled her face away from Teacup's enthusiastic licking.

"Then you shouldn't have unfriended him."

"Claire. Please. We've discussed this." Portions of the story anyway.

"We've barely scratched the surface."

Janie twisted her lips. Claire didn't agree with how vigorously Janie had yanked out the plug and then drained the tub on her and Keon's relationship. After all, last summer, she and Keon had parted on amiable terms. Or so she'd tried to convince herself.

Two months before the split, when they'd decided to see each other outside of the friend group after falling into bed one steamy night, they'd declared their relationship fun and light. Certainly nothing deep or emotional. They were supposed to have been together for a "good time, not a long time," lyrics Keon had quoted from a classic Canadian rock song. There was no sense in either of them becoming attached with only eight weeks remaining in his stay.

Or so she'd told herself.

Both she and he had supposedly understood that he would finish his stint researching organic farming in the US before leaving to run Hamaguchi's in a stunning, lake-strewn valley in British Columbia. Where he would live out his rewarding, prosperous days without her.

But...as Janie had learned...it was one thing to glimpse updates on Keon's hobbies and relationships on her friends' phones. It was quite another to view post after post glowing from her own screen. About his family. About his business. About his string of girlfriends.

Teacup jumped around on her lap. Janie settled the dog with soothing strokes.

Claire planted a hand on her hip. "Keon is flying

in Thursday night. Four days from now. Then you can check in with him—in person—about anything you want."

"Yes. You're right, Claire. I'm sorry." But would Janie accept another online friend request from her ex following the wedding? Not if she wanted to recover from the lingering bruising on her heart and find someone to love for real throughout her fulfilling but empty life.

Claire gestured toward the sliding glass door leading into Mrs. Hoyt's home. "I heard a car pull up when Teacup and I were near the fence. Heath must be here. I don't want Tania's mom throwing a hissy fit thinking we're lounging around soaking up rays while the others work on the name-place cards."

Heath was Trey's younger brother and the best man for next weekend's wedding. Janie and Claire were bridesmaids. Claire, as maid of honor, had been paired with Heath. Janie ranked as bridesmaid number two, while Keon occupied four out of five in the groomsmen lineup. A flower girl and a button-cute ring bearer completed the wedding party. The numbers veered into overkill if anyone asked Janie, although her bosses at Sunshine & Roses were thrilled about handling the floral arrangements.

Getting up, she set down Teacup and passed the

dog the satin bone. Claire retrieved the tied-off bag and stuffed the waste into a diminutive trashcan reserved for the purpose.

Teacup trotted toward the glass door, pink hairbow bouncing.

"At your service, milady," Janie quipped, gliding open the door. She and Claire trailed the Yorkie into the massive rec room. Teacup dropped her bone and romped toward the wet bar at the room's far end. Tania, a petite redhead, squealed and scooped the dog into her arms, welcoming Yorkie kisses.

Janie surveyed the room. The scene had transformed in the twenty minutes since she and Claire took Teacup outside. Two hours ago, every bridesmaid except for an overworked Alicia had assembled at Mrs. Hoyt's house for snacks and wedding preparations, along with the good-natured groom. Now, not one person decorated the reception name-place cards at the long folding table. Lively music flowed from ceiling speakers, and a party mood filled the space.

Janie swapped a glance with Claire. "What's going on?" she whispered.

Claire shrugged. "Beats me."

"Janie," Tania called, flinging up a hand and racing over with Teacup. "You'll never guess what happened." Tania bounced on her heels, and the Yorkie's head bobbled.

"What?" The event must be out of the ordinary, because Tania's high-strung mother did not tolerate shenanigans beneath her roof. Mrs. Hoyt prided herself on presiding over her guests with an imperious gaze and eleven thousand rules of conduct. Yet even Mrs. H. preened, patting her hair and pursing her lips. Trey, the groom, clapped his younger brother, Heath, on the back.

Tania squeaked. "Heath surprised Trey! I hope you don't mind."

"Why would I mind?" Janie cast another glance toward the wet bar. Heath held court, smiling and nursing a beer. Near the refrigerator, Tania's two sisters giggled. Then the sisters stepped aside, and —Janie wobbled on her kitten heels—*Keon* emerged.

The blood rushed out of her face. "What's he doing here?" she whispered to Claire. Eyes snapping wider than a Chucky doll's, she gaped at Tania. "What's *he* doing here?" Four days early!

Giant white dots speckled her vision. She slapped a hand to her galloping heart. She had begrudgingly accepted that Keon's presence during the wedding rehearsal this Friday night and the nuptials Saturday afternoon would storm a major assault on her senses. Over the last week, she had pep-talked herself through the awkwardness of encountering him at Sunday's present-opening. But *no one* had breathed a word about the possibility of her coming face-to-face with Keon Rivers today.

Not before Friday.

His dark brown gaze meandered in her direction. He strolled past Mrs. H., stroking his chin in a maddeningly thoughtful manner.

Janie's molars clomped together. "What are you doing here?"

"Hello to you too, Janie," Keon replied in a deep, husky voice that spun sensual awareness along her arms and down her legs. And everywhere in between. "You look incredible."

The liar. Yorkie slobber speckled the neckline of her top, and a blob of powdered-donut jelly stained her skirt from an unfortunate incident at the deco-rating table.

Keon smiled, his white teeth dazzling against his tanned skin. Janie's knees buckled.

Claire gripped her arm. "She's going down!"

"No, I'm not." Janie jostled off her friend's grasp. She was *not* swooning because Keon Too-Sexy-for-

His-T-shirt-and-Cargo-Shorts Rivers had shown up in her life almost out of the blue.

She pulled herself together. She was on top of her game. She was in control.

Janie McAllister didn't swoon for any man, let alone the only guy in her twenty-seven years who had pleasantly, politely, and unwittingly broken her heart.

Chapter Two

KEON RIVERS HADN'T an inkling what reaction he'd expected from Janie McAllister upon encountering his former girlfriend for the first time in a year. Call him optimistic, but the dismay—or was that disdain?—on her face and in her voice hadn't crossed his mind.

He reached toward her as she recovered from her stumble. "You okay?"

Her hand shot up, palm out. "My fault. I wasn't watching where I was going." She brushed a strand of sandy-blond hair over her shoulder and laced her fingers in front of her skirt. Her gray-blue eyes, the magnificent shade of cloudy skies right before a driving rain, challenged him to question the veracity of her statement.

As in, he had better *not*.

Keon peeked at the floor. Nothing marred the surrounding tile at her sandaled feet. He would bet the fifty Canadian bucks not exactly burning a hole in his wallet that his presence in Mrs. Hoyt's house had knocked Janie for a loop. In hindsight, accepting Heath Whitaker's invitation to arrive in Greater Seattle a few days early might not have been his wisest course of action.

But here he was. On Sunday afternoon instead of this Thursday night. Big deal. Janie would have to deal with it. *Deal with me.*

And not pretend to cut him out of her life, like she had with surgical precision since they'd broken up. After their amazing summer together, he hadn't understood why she'd believed a complete split necessary. Yeah, they'd made a pact of sorts to assign an expiration date to their...situationship. Sure, he lived in BC while she lived in Washington, but people shared long-distance romances all the time. Until they didn't. But she'd simply decided after their last intimate morning in bed to call it quits. No fanfare. No tears. Just...we're done.

What the hell? He'd believed, however foolishly considering he hadn't spoken the words, that she'd known how he'd felt, how he'd *loved her*. Even if falling head over hiking boots was unexpected and unplanned.

Janie hadn't wanted to hear about an 'international affair,' as she'd termed the concept. There had been no waterworks at the airport. Just a single tear dribbling down her cheek, a tight hug, a quick kiss, and a quickly voiced, "See ya."

Beside a statue-still Janie, Claire Merriweather smiled. "Hi, Keon." Claire enveloped him in a friendly embrace. "It's great to see you."

"Same, Claire. You look good."

"So do you."

Next, he shared a hug with Tania Hoyt, the bride. Tania cradled her small dog to one side. "Thank you for surprising us," Tania said.

"My pleasure."

Janie's gaze darted between her two friends. "Yes," she chirped. "This is so great." She inched toward Keon and opened her arms as if she were about to cuddle a grizzly bear.

Keon grinned. "Ah, Janie. I've missed you." Her quirkiness and sparkle. Her devotion to her friends and family. In the year since he'd flown home, he hadn't met another woman like her. And he had tried. "Come here." He spread his arms wider than hers. Could he help it if he had longer limbs?

She wet her lips. Sending her friends a wary glance, she moved forward.

Keon wrapped her in a close hug. He shut his eyes, and his breath stopped for a heart-pounding moment. She smelled incredible. Like fresh air and flowers and precious, precious Janie.

He'd longed for her scent, the rightness of her in his arms. He'd longed to hold her again. To hold her and hold her and never, ever stop.

A puff of air feathered against his neck. A sound of contentment he recognized from their sexy times reached his ears. Then her shoulders stiffened, and Tania's voice pierced his Janie-haze.

"Isn't this wonderful?" Tania set down her dog, and Keon and Janie broke apart. The pooch scampered toward the wet bar. Tania beamed. "The entire group, getting back together."

"For your wedding," Janie stressed. "No other reason."

"Speak for yourself," Keon whispered, hiding a small smile behind a finger.

"I am," she whispered back, her dark blond eyebrows dipping into a pretty V.

Keon noticed everyone watching them. Their mutual friends, Tania's two younger sisters, and Tania's mother, gathered in a loose circle. As did

Trey and Heath, the Whitaker brothers, Keon's buddies since the trio met as teens during respective family vacations in Hawaii.

Janie cleared her throat. "We're all doing so, so wonderful. Glad we straightened that out." She ran a hand from her collarbone to the side of her neck. Then she blinked, dropping both hands and interlocking her fingers again.

Claire nudged her. "This one has news," she said to Keon. "Go on. Tell him."

The furrows on Janie's forehead deepened. "Tell him what?"

"That Sunshine & Roses is doing the wedding flowers. And you're assistant manager there now. Plus, the owners want you to take over when they retire." Claire gave Keon a look. "In two years."

A saccharine smile tipped Janie's mouth. "I don't have to tell him. You've covered it. My riveting achievements in a nutshell. Hooray for me."

Hope kindled in Keon's heart. Neither Janie nor Claire had mentioned a guy.

Mrs. Hoyt clapped her hands. Once. Loudly. "Attention, everyone! Keon, you must be famished." Mrs. H. turned to her youngest daughter. "Noni, please bring in the charcuterie board."

"I have to go to the bathroom," Noni protested. "Why can't Tami do it?"

Mrs. H. clucked her tongue. "Honestly, Wynona, it's not like I'm asking you to construct a new Space Needle. Attend to your personal needs and *then* fetch the platter." Mrs. H. smiled at Tami, her middle daughter. "Tams will check on Mr. Sprinkles." The family's huge, hairy cat. She patted Tami's hand. "Thank you, dear. The poor boy gets skittish when the house is full."

Noni flounced down the hall. Tami followed close behind.

Mrs. H. and the others drifted away, leaving Keon and Janie standing beside the craft table overflowing with wedding decorations.

"So," Janie began in a polite voice, her gaze hovering to land around his ear and not his eyes. "You came early."

He nodded. "It was Heath's idea. Tania is stressed, and Trey feels like this wedding is snowballing into an episode of terrible reality TV. I'm here to help with last-minute tasks so the bride and groom can relax. Getting married should be a joyous occasion." The pandemonium Heath had described sounded horrific.

Janie flicked her fingers. "I hear you. When I get

married, we'll have maybe one or two attendants per side and only our family and closest friends at the reception."

"*Our?*" Keon's pulse thundered. "Are you engaged?"

"What?" Her eyes widened. "That came out wrong." Red spots flared high on her cheeks. "No," she stated. "Not engaged. I'm nowhere near that point in my life. I'm not even dating right now. You know how it is. Working, working, working. Can't remember the last time I loaded a dating app, much less swiped."

The death-grip on Keon's chest released. She hadn't found someone. *Excellent.* Not that he didn't want her to be happy. He did. He wanted all her dreams to come true. But he also wanted another chance to see if they were right for each other.

Not for a summer. For the long haul.

"Most women dream about their wedding day from the time they're little, right? Janie, if you were serious about someone, what would you picture? The ceremony, for example." An assortment of Okanagan Valley venues paraded through his mind. Many of his buddies and extended family members were tying the knot. He'd attended his fair share of weddings before and after his year in Washington, including one in the middle of this past January. The ceremony had taken place on the balcony of a hillside resort overlooking a dramatic gorge. The bride wore a faux-fur-trimmed wedding cloak over a striking winter wedding gown Janie would rock.

"I dunno," she replied, lifting a shoulder. "A beach? A park?"

"A beach sounds nice." Preferably lakeside. "How about a vineyard?"

Her chin tucked in. She eyed him sideways. "Can we talk about something else?"

"Yeah, yeah." Keon's face warmed. What had come over him? He was a business owner, not an event planner.

Janie glanced toward the wet bar. "Wow, I'm parched. I could use a glass of wine." She stepped away. "How are your parents?" she asked over her shoulder as she headed toward their friends.

A high-pitched feline death howl erupted from the hall, curtailing Keon's response. Mrs. Hoyt's cat streaked into the rec room in a blur of black, white, and orange fur. Tania's tiny dog careened past her mother's legs in full pursuit of the cat.

Mrs. Hoyt screeched. Her wine goblet skidded out of her hand, shattering on the tiles. Shards of crystal and rosé spewed at the woman's feet.

Tania gasped. "Teacup!"

The Yorkie chased the wailing cat beneath the craft table. The feline arched its spine and hissed.

Trey grabbed a cloth from the bar. "Keon," he shouted, crouching at the mess. "Open the door!"

"Let the cat into the yard," Janie clarified, catching Teacup and lifting the excited dog. "I have this girl."

Keon whipped open the sliding glass panel. Mr. Sprinkles yowled, escaping onto the patio and the yard beyond.

"Crisis averted," he said, closing the glass.

Teacup barked from the protection of Janie's embrace. The animal's pink hairbow drooped.

"Shush, imp," Janie murmured in a caring voice, looking beautiful in her light blue top and floral skirt, despite a dollop resembling strawberry jam on the fabric near her hip.

An ache built behind Keon's sternum as he imagined Janie holding a child with chubby, jam-smeared cheeks. *Their* child. A little girl with his dark hair and her cute nose—and attitude to spare.

Their gazes caught. For a second, their end of the rec room exuded a soothing oasis vibe in a space buzzing with conversation and activity and the rapid breathing of a tuckered Yorkie. Except Janie was probably brainstorming ways to evade Keon's presence, much like Mr. Sprinkles had bolted from the house. Whereas he could stand here drinking in the sight of her for hours.

Noni returned, carting the charcuterie board. She positioned the platter on the bar and invited the group to dig in. Heath selected olives, cheese, and crackers, placing his eats on a paper napkin.

Tami appeared in the archway, eyes huge. "Mom! The centerpieces are ruined!"

Bea Hoyt whirled to face her middle daughter. *"What?"*

Keon's ears rang.

"I was checking on Mr. Sprinkles." Tami's voice shook. "I thought he was sleeping on the cat perch in the spare room where we keep the centerpieces. The decorations reek of cat pee."

Mrs. H. splayed her fingers, arms stretching toward the ceiling as if she were beseeching Zeus to put her out of her misery and smite her already. "I cannot stand it! Not for another minute."

Keon stared at Janie. "What in the world—?"

Tania burst into tears. Trey cradled his fiancée against his chest, rubbing Tania's shoulders and kissing her hair.

Claire took over cleaning the glass debris with a broom and dustpan.

Janie met Keon's gaze around the Yorkie's head. "The centerpieces were for the reception," she whispered. "They're quite intricate. Lovely handmade paper flowers in cardstock vases. Tania designed them."

"Okay," Keon said, motioning toward Tania's mom as the fifty-something woman wrestled control of her outburst, pacing and mumbling about cats and dogs and absentminded daughters. "But this reaction seems overboard."

"This wedding has been one disaster after another," Janie responded in hushed tones. "Tania and the dog have been staying here, away from Trey the last couple of weeks, to make the wedding night special."

Keon whispered, "As in, the bride and groom haven't been doing *it*?"

"Yeah."

"Huh. Interesting concept." Considering Trey and Tania lived together.

"A lot of couples spend time apart before the ceremony," Janie said.

"I'll take your word on that."

"It's common wedding protocol. Although

maybe not for that length of time." Adjusting Teacup's hairbow, she looked away.

Tania's sobs subsided. She faced the group. "We need to fix this."

Trey looped an arm around his fiancée. "How many centerpieces were destroyed?" he asked Tania's middle sister. "One? Two?"

Tami's freckles stood out in stark relief against her pale skin. "All twelve."

Heath waited in the background, finishing his snack.

Claire swept up the last of the glass shards.

"I'll redo the centerpieces," Janie volunteered.

"Aw," Tania said, sending Keon's ex a watery smile. "Thank you, Janie. You're sweet. But you have too much on your plate this week." She sighed. "Mom?"

Mrs. Hoyt inhaled. "Your sisters and I will whip up replacements, sweetheart. Don't worry." Mrs. H. paused. "Tania. Dear. I know I promised to look after Teacup until you return from honeymoon, but we might want to make other arrangements."

Keon frowned. "How do we know the cat wrecked the decorations?" He didn't want to blame the Yorkie, but the likelihood loomed. "What about the dog?" He indicated Janie and the perky pooch.

Noni piped up. "Trust me. Cat spray has a distinct odor."

"It's not Teacup's fault," Claire said, setting aside the broom and dustpan.

"She's an apartment dog," Janie added. "She's not used to cats and tons of rooms." She kissed Teacup's head, and Keon's heart tumbled over in his chest.

"Can I have her?" he asked.

With a shrug, Janie passed him the dog.

Teacup licked his nose, and he laughed. "She's cute." He gazed into the tiny animal's brown eyes. "You didn't mean to scare Bea's—I mean, Mrs. H.'s cat, did you?"

The dog blinked, looking as innocent as a 1930s bank robber.

Mrs. H. smiled. "You can call me Bea, Keon. I feel ancient when you kids call me Mrs., but it's a habit for some of Tania's childhood friends."

He grinned over the dog's head. "Got it."

Heath wandered over, dusting his hands on his napkin. "Is T-Dog going home with Trey, then?"

"I don't see how that will work," Tania replied, gaze narrowing as she pondered.

Trey offered a kind smile. "It's fine."

"But honey, you're grinding out hours to make up for our honeymoon."

Bea released a breath. "Tania. Sweetheart. Be reasonable. My nerves are frayed. Your dog is chasing Mr. Sprinkles. She's chasing the cat next door. On our walks, she strains her harness, sniffing for the cat around the block."

Teacup sat up taller in Keon's arms.

Heath balled his napkin and stuffed the wad into a pocket of his shorts. "Dudes. Problem solved. Keon and I will take the dog. Right, Kee? Kee is sleeping on my couch until his room is ready at the wedding hotel. That's not until Thursday. What else you got going on?" Heath elbowed Keon.

"Nothing much." Other than helping prevent more wedding fiascoes and coming to grips with the realization over these last several months that Janie McAllister might very well be the love of his life.

Chapter Three

Janie stifled a yawn and tucked a big-buttoned sunflower into a cheerful vase of hot-pink dahlias and soft-purple delphiniums. She shifted her feet on a cushioned floor mat at her design station in the back storage room of Sunshine & Roses.

Not for the first time on this dreary, cloudy Monday, she whispered a few words of gratitude that her boss, Roslyn Murdoch, had elected to spend the morning up front. It wouldn't do for Janie to expose their customers to her gloominess. The store's philosophy revolved around ensuring every shopper went away feeling uplifted, not leave them digging around in the doldrums like a mangy groundhog despairing of ever seeing his shadow again.

"Now, Janie, you're not in the doldrums," she lectured herself. It was her darn imaginary groundhog. And lack of sleep. Who could have predicted that encountering Keon at the craft party yesterday would plague her as she'd tossed and turned? So what if he'd come to town early? Without so much as a, "Hey, Heath, let's text Tania and tell her we're on our way over. While we're at it, maybe we should ask her to alert Janie."

So. What?

Janie stuffed another sunflower into the arrangement, selected greenery, and snipped off the ends. It wasn't like she needed to have anything to do with Keon until Friday. There was no *Seeing Your Ex Again* handbook with helpful hints on how to handle the situation. Was there? No rule requiring she obsess about how handsome and sexy and kind and considerate he had looked holding Teacup.

And what was up with him quizzing her about the sort of wedding *she* might want? Their curious conversation had instigated her anxiety dreams about marrying *him*!

That would never happen. He was Canadian. She was American. He was fond of maple leaves, and she saluted the Stars and Stripes. He managed an established family business, and she intended to oversee Sunshine & Roses. Her bosses were counting on her.

Myriad thoughts swirled in her mind, a common occurrence while she created. Concentrating on her task, she sunk her teeth into her lower lip. Strictly speaking, becoming a florist didn't require an advanced degree. A design certificate, some college classes, common sense, courtesy, an artistic flair, and a passion for inflicting joy were positives. But if a tsunami swept her into a sodden grave while she sunbathed comatose on the beach, the Murdochs could hire and train someone else.

She poked more stems into the vase. A fresh, outdoorsy scent filled the air.

Taking the academic exercise of her exhaustion-fueled fantasy to the extreme, even if she remained in Rosevale to manage the shop, a one-hour flight from Seattle departed twice daily for Kelowna, near where Keon lived. Technically, if he didn't have a girlfriend and considered Janie as more than a fling from last summer, they might trial-run an international affair.

Do you really believe what you felt for him amounted to a fling?

She flinched at the unwelcome thought before glancing around the backroom. Had her imaginary groundhog stuck his head out of a burrow and spied sunbeams? Was the critter an eternal optimist?

Because where could a long-distance relationship with Keon lead? Why bother daydreaming? Why set herself up for another dose of pain and heartache?

Stepping back from the design station, she studied her handiwork. "Oh, boy." Numerous sprigs of fragrant myrtle, far too many boughs of leatherleaf fern, and a withered batch of lemon leaf protruded from the vase, overwhelming the blossoms.

She puffed out a breath. "See, Keon Rivers?" she muttered. "This is what you do to my peace of mind." He mixed it up.

She extracted the sprigs. Her phone beeped from beside the bunches of greenery. A message from Heath Whitaker appeared on the screen:

> Dudette. Clerk busted a wrist. I gotta step in.

Janie examined the message, chewing the inside of her cheek. Trey's younger brother Heath was long on looks but short on communication skills. Was he saying he needed to work at his skateboard shop instead of driving Janie to a wholesale club to buy essentials for Tania and Trey's new condo? She *didn't* have to babysit the groom's well-intentioned but scatterbrained brother during one of their assigned wedding errands?

This day was looking up!

She texted back:

> Not a problem. I can do alone. Will borrow the Sunshine van.

> My truck avail. Sending my subdue.

Janie shook her head. *Subdue?* she texted.

> Ha! Sub dude.

Her brow wrinkled. Sub dude? Heath's substitute dude? One of his friends? Or another groomsman?

Oh, God. Not Keon! She gulped. She hadn't wrapped her head around the man's surprise visit yet.

Her thumbs flew on her phone:

> Heath! No need for stud dude. I can mange—

Cursing autocorrect, she backspaced.

"Oh, Janie!" The shop's owner, Roslyn Murdoch, called from somewhere in the store. Roslyn's lively voice preceded the woman's arrival into the back-room. "Your ride is here."

Janie plunked down her phone. *No, no, no!* Heath wouldn't do this to her. He wasn't that dense.

Except he was.

Pulse zipping in her veins like an anxiety-ridden goldfish bumping the inside of its bowl, she turned. Several feet from the entrance into the storage room, Roslyn stood beside a smiling Keon.

Janie's heart leaped. Then she remembered the pointlessness of allowing her heart to leap and stifled her response to her handsome ex.

He took a step closer. "Hey, Janie," he said softly.

"Hey." Her mouth dried. Could he *see* her pulse bopping beneath her skin?

Roslyn folded her hands. "Keon and his family are opening a floral department at their garden center in British Columbia. I've been giving him dozens of tips these past few months."

"Roslyn knows her stuff," Keon confirmed as Janie's boss stepped to the design station and inspected the dahlia order.

Janie resisted the urge to shake her head. "Wh-what? You two have been talking?"

"Yeah." Keon nodded.

Her brain fogged. During his year in Washington, Janie and he had discussed Hamaguchi's providing fresh floral arrangements as part of a planned expansion. Yet Keon hadn't thought to ask *her* for advice? The disappointment stung.

His shoulders lifted. He glanced away as if uncomfortable saying more in front of her boss. "I would have asked you about it, Janie, but you know..."

"Actually, I don't."

His brown gaze penetrated her, and his meaning clocked her on the forehead. *Right.* She'd severed all ties. *Sheesh.*

Still, he could have reached out via one of their mutual friends. And she would have done—what?

What *would* she have done?

"A floral department is a fabulous idea," she said, easy-breezy-like. "So, you're Heath's stud dude?"

A laugh tumbled out of his mouth. "Sorry?"

"Sub. Uh, sub. Uh, substitute dude." The heat of a blush wormed up her neck.

Roslyn picked through the discarded greenery. "Janie? Are you done?"

Oh, she was done. So was this embarrassing exchange. "Roslyn, can we have some privacy?"

The woman nodded. "I'll finish the order after you leave." Roslyn returned to the front of the store.

Keon slipped his hands into the back pockets of his dark jeans, which hugged his lower body in all the right places. "Janie, if this feels awkward for you, I can go."

"Yes." She mentally skipped her feet in a victory jig. "That would be awesome."

A scowl marred his striking features. "Really? That's how you want to play today?"

She didn't want to *play*. That was the point. In the end, she'd wanted far more from Keon than a good time for a short time, even if she hadn't fully comprehended the depth of her feelings until after he'd left. She arched her eyebrows. "Why did you ask if you didn't want to know?" She sounded prickly, but erecting walls against his sexy sincerity topped revealing the soft pulp of her heart.

He turned up a hand. "I was being polite."

"That's a problem. You're kind. You're nice. You're a difficult man to say no to."

His lips twitched. "You don't seem to have an issue."

She crossed her arms, staring at him. A tiny fissure cracked open in her defenses, darn it.

"Can we talk for a minute first?" he asked.

She held in a breath. She was being ridiculous. Keon wasn't a threat to her peace of mind unless she allowed him to become one. He didn't understand that his departure had ripped her heart into several ragged, throbbing pieces. From his perspective, they'd enjoyed each other's company for a couple of months, then parted on an agreed-upon date. Nice and tidy. Zero complications.

Neither of them had expected her emotions to run amok.

In fact, *he* didn't realize they had. She'd kept that unsettling tidbit to herself.

"This situation isn't about me," he said. "It's not about us. It's about Tania and Trey—"

"And their wedding." Janie blew a hair out of her face. "I know."

His forehead creased. "I didn't plan to just waltz in here. Heath said he'd text, seeing as I can't without ditching my phone number for one you haven't blocked."

"Heath did text," Janie admitted, ignoring the dig about how she'd annihilated Keon from her digital life. She deserved the barb. "His message showed up seconds before you and Roslyn came in. What can I say? You caught me by surprise."

"Okay. Well, I parked Heath's truck in the lot as instructed. I knocked on the service door like he said." Keon pointed to the door eight feet from her design station. "No one answered. That's when I entered the shop from the front sidewalk and saw Roslyn. She said you were preparing an order." His finger swung to the monitor above the door separating the storage and design areas from the floral displays and cash counter. "There are cameras everywhere. Roslyn and I talked for ten minutes. I thought, any second now Janie will check the monitor and notice me."

She scratched her neck, glancing down. "I was deep in thought."

"You lose yourself in your work. I get that. What I don't understand is why you're treating me like I'm carrying an infectious disease."

Pursing her lips, Janie moseyed to the shelves stocked with an assortment of vases, ribbons, and florist paraphernalia. One eye on Keon, she smoothed a fingertip along a spool of two-inch-wide emerald-green satin. Flipping up the unsecured end of the roll, she squared off the fabric and slipped it into place.

"Keon, this complication today with Heath seems suspicious. And convenient." She curled a strand of shoulder-length hair behind one ear and faced her ex in his ultra-fine stud-dudeness. "His clerk gets injured, and you need to take his place on a shopping trip I can manage myself?" Although she had looked forward to Heath flexing his muscles rather than her breaking her back wheeling heavy trays of canned goods into the warehouse-club parking lot, depositing the groceries into his truck bed, and hefting out the flats again at Tania and Trey's new building. "Can't you see? It's a classic setup." Janie should know. She'd taken part in the activity often enough.

Keon's gaze narrowed. "To what end?"

"To force us to spend time together."

"Force us? How about *wanting* to? I'm only here a few days. I'd hoped we could catch up."

She rolled her eyes. "Keon, you have a girlfriend."

The corners of his mouth curved. "Keeping tabs on me?"

"Tania mentioned a name in passing. Donna? Danielle?" Shaking her head, Janie feigned puzzlement. "Something with a D."

"Danika." Keon grinned. "We split."

She swallowed. *News to me!* Regarding his single status. Not the woman's name.

"If my coming to Sunshine & Roses is a dastardly plot, it's not Heath's doing," Keon said. "His clerk fractured a bone at the skatepark. I saw the cast at the skate store after meeting Derek and his new girlfriend at Alicia Maxwell's cupcake shop. Cute place, by the way."

A peculiar sensation slithered down Janie's spine. "You contacted my brother? When?"

"Last night. We had coffee this morning."

She cringed. Why hadn't Derek or Lacey passed on this critical scrap of information? Had Derek peered into her soul during a weak moment when Janie had let her defenses slip?

Keon tossed his hands in the air. "What was I supposed to do, Janie? End half my friendships because you took the concept of ghosting to an extreme?"

When he put it like that, she came off as spiteful. "I needed to make a clean break."

"And I need to make it through this wedding with you and I being civil to each other." Pacing the floor beside the sunflower arrangement, he raked a hand through his black hair. The ends stood up. The muss looked far too sexy on him. He glanced at her.

"When Derek and I had a moment alone, he said you destroyed our garden."

"He *what*?" Janie plastered her hands to her face. She peeped at Keon from between her fingers. The nerve of her twin!

"Our garden," Keon repeated in a clear voice, as if she were an automated telephone answering system continually patching him through to the wrong department. "That you and I planted in the raised beds on your apartment rooftop last spring? He said you weed-whacked the flowers after I left."

Janie gasped. "That was personal!" And private. Damn Derek. She lowered her hands.

"Personal against me?" Keon asked.

"No. I promise." Not against *him*. Against her run-amok emotions. "I was feeling PMS-ish." Sensitive and crabby. "I felt bad afterward." Absolutely aghast. "But the damage was done. It's kind of hard to take back weed-whacking." She folded her arms over her short-sleeved blouse. "Still. My brother had no right."

Keon pulled a pleated paper napkin out of his jeans pocket. He strode over and handed her the napkin. "Derek asked me to give you this."

Janie opened the soft paper and glimpsed a sketch of a wicked-looking smiley face complete with devil horns she recognized from the cartoons her brother had scribbled all over her middle school notebooks. Underneath the drawing, her twin's scrawl declared:

Payback...big sis. Opportunity knocks. Deal with your crap.

Her jaw tightened. Derek had probably written the note in retaliation for Janie's elaborate match-making of him and Lacey ten days ago. He only called her 'big sis' when he wanted to make her howl at the moon with frustration. But Derek and Lacey were happy. He should send her a gigantic box of chocolates, not a payback message.

She folded the napkin into a fat square, asking Keon, "Did you read this?"

"Why would I? Like you said, it's personal."

"Good. Thanks." Janie slipped the note into her bra. She would verbally bop her four-minutes-younger brother on the head later.

She looked at Keon again, and he let out a rough exhale. Stomach clenching, she touched his hand. His skin warmed her chilly fingertips.

"I'm sorry," she murmured. "Destroying our flowerbed was an awful act of destruction and…and…" Her chest squeezed tight as she searched for the right words.

"Hurt?" Keon pressed.

"Yes," Janie agreed. "And I'm sorry you had to learn about the weed-whacking from my brother."

Keon interlaced their fingers, and her pulse resumed its chaotic pace.

"I got the impression Derek wants us to hash things out," he said, squeezing her hands. "That he believes there might be unresolved feelings on both our parts. Telling me about the weed-whacking gave me an excuse to touch base with you, Janie," he added in a kind voice.

"But you were coming to Sunshine anyway," she whispered. Because that was Keon. If a friend—in this case, Heath—needed a hand, he readily offered.

"Yes." He nodded. "I was coming." His gaze probed hers, and her heart pinched. "The guys on the groomsmen text chain have been dancing around the subject of our breakup for months," he said quietly. "They're not the only ones wondering if we ended things too soon."

Her breath caught. "We followed our relationship guidelines."

"It doesn't matter. That's in the past. We have today, and I want to spend time with you, Janie."

Tears burned her eyes. "Keon, it will only hurt that much more when you fly home again." In one week.

A troubled look passed over his face. "I've missed you, Janie. Haven't you missed me? Not even a little?"

"Of course I have." Or she wouldn't have torpedoed their flowerbed, a symbolic but ultimately futile attempt to deflect her agony and protect her heart. A heart that still required guarding. Between the pair of them, she wasn't the one who had plunged into a new relationship four weeks after their split. Although by then she had thwarted Keon's attempts to stay in touch.

She tightened her hold on his fingers. "Keon," she whispered, every fiber of her body throbbing. "What we had was wonderful. But there are too many obstacles standing in our way to risk picking things up again."

He smiled. "We can crush obstacles."

Releasing his hand, she shook her head. "Our relationship was supposed to be simple and easy. And I—I need to focus on this wedding." She rubbed her temples. She needed to muster the fortitude to suffer through standing in three-inch-high heels in the bridesmaid line across from Keon and the other groomsmen at the church altar. Steel herself against her heart swelling with gooey sentiment at the handsome sight of this generous man in a custom-fitted, dark-gray suit. Shield her tender emotions from the intensity of her response to him as they interacted at the reception and again at the gift-opening the following day.

Then—the greatest hardship—to say goodbye to him again. She closed her mind to the possibility of his week in Rosevale ending any other way.

He brushed a thumb across his lower lip. "Janie…"

Her phone rang on the design table. She stepped onto the mat and scanned the screen. "It's Tania. She usually texts." Which meant this call was important. "I should answer."

"Go ahead. Pick up." Keon swiped a hand over the tired lines of his face and walked to the supply shelves.

Faking a cheerful voice, Janie tapped the icon. "Howdy, happiest woman in the world. What's up?"

Tania spoke in a rush. "I heard Keon is taking on Heath's wedding tasks. Janie, I'm sorry. I wouldn't have cornered you with him like that."

"It's okay," Janie responded. "I know you wouldn't have." Mostly, other than leaning on her brother's shoulder a time or two, she had kept her heartache to herself. However, out of her girlfriends, she had confided in Tania the most.

"Heath feels horrible that he can't help with the condo stuff," Tania said. "His poor clerk is out of commission for the rest of the week."

"Don't worry. It's not an issue."

Tania groaned. "If anything else goes wrong before Saturday, I swear I'm calling off the wedding. Trey and I should have eloped! All these mess-ups are so frustrating."

"Tania, take a breath." Janie blinked. Was this what weddings did to couples? She darted a glance across the room. Keon stood near a shelf of vases, his hands on his hips and his head down. Was he worn out? Feeling ill? Dangling from the end of his rope?

The bride's voice bounced off her eardrum. "Now that Heath is out of commission, please let Keon help with your wedding tasks. It would mean so much to Trey and me."

The hairs on the back of Janie's neck stiffened. "Come again?" she whispered into her phone. Had she been right? Was something afoot? Were her friends and brother conspiring against her, setting up her and Keon? She could accomplish the list of wedding chores alone. Hire someone online to help. Enlist the aid of a Hoyt sister.

Except, this week, Janie was Tania's go-to girl. Whatever the bride needed, no matter what Tania asked, Janie had pre-volunteered. Every bridesmaid, including Tania's sisters, had taken a turn. Confident the busy work would distract her from Keon's visit, Janie had requested *this* specific span of days. Her brilliant brainwave suddenly dumped into brain dumb.

"It won't be all the time," Tania added, a note of desperation creeping into her voice. "Only when you need those extra hands."

Images of Keon's large hands and dexterous fingers caressing every inch of Janie's body brimmed to overflowing in the bubbling brooks of her mind.

Glancing at her ex-boyfriend again, she whispered into the phone. "I don't know if I can handle the, um, exposure, if you get my drift. What if my soft spot"—for Keon—"gets mushy?" What if the emotions she'd worked so hard to bury clambered to the surface, reflecting in her eyes and slipping off her tongue?

"Janie, please." Tania's fretful tones reverberated in her ear. "I'm overwhelmed, and there's too much for you to do alone. Marrying Trey—I mean, *of course*

I'm marrying Trey. Why wouldn't I go through with our wedding?"

Janie froze. *Oh-oh.* Trying to appear nonchalant in case Keon glanced over, she twirled a strand of hair around a finger and moved to the furthest recesses of the room. "Tania?" she murmured into her phone. "Are you okay?"

"I think I am," her friend replied. "I'm giving it everything I've got. But this wedding—everything is unraveling. All our plans. Our dreams. What if Trey and I unravel too?" Tania's voice emitted from the phone in convulsive gasps. "We're supposed to be starting our brand-new lives. In our brand-new condo. With our brand-new furniture. A brand-new couch. Brand-new bed. Brand-new sheets! Brand-new towels. Brand-new dishes. Brand-new pots and pans! Everything shiny and new. But *I* don't feel shiny. I feel bedraggled."

Janie's mouth dropped open. Her concerns about spending time with Keon paled compared to the hellish case of frozen foot-sicles Tania described.

She placed a hand on her chest, and the folded napkin in her bra flattened. She couldn't stand to bear responsibility for the bride falling apart and maybe even skipping out on the groom days before their wedding. Janie wanted her friend to walk down the aisle this Saturday feeling nothing but certainty and love for the wonderful life she and Trey would share. From the top of Tania's beautiful head of red hair bedecked with a gorgeous veil to her extravagant wedding gown, Janie's friend deserved to enjoy every second of her special day. And to cherish the moments and memories leading up to the nuptials.

If that meant Janie needed to risk swerving a bit too close to the dazzling heat of Keon's flame and pray she didn't get scorched again, then that was what she would do.

She cast another glance at his handsome profile. Her heart banged. Her throat dried, and her lungs burned.

That *was* what a good friend would do.

Right?

Chapter Four

KEON MONITORED the busy afternoon traffic in the side mirrors of the red sports pickup he'd borrowed from Heath. Following his phone's directions to Trey and Tania's new condo, he steered around a corner and sent a glance toward Janie in the passenger seat.

A line formed on her forehead as she studied wedding tasks on her own device. Groceries stuffed the floorboard around her sandals, and Teacup peeked from a padded canine carrier secured to the center console, the only spot for the tiny dog, who, Janie had said, suffered motion sickness and needed the freedom to survey her surroundings. At Tania's request, Keon and Janie had retrieved the animal from Heath's place following their trip to the whole-sale club. Tania hadn't wanted the dog trapped inside her future brother-in-law's apartment until Heath got home from work.

Keon cast another glance Janie's way, and a familiar wave of heat rolled through him. He hadn't expected to miss her so much when he'd left Rosevale. Now, only Teacup separated them in the truck's cab, and he *still* missed her.

"You're quiet," he said. "Is something wrong?" Other than the obvious issue of needing to deal with his unexpected presence.

A carefree mask slid over her features. "No. Not at all." Her hand batted an invisible speck in the air. "Everything is A-okay." She tapped her phone screen. "Condo-stocking trip," she read from her list. "Done. Packing stuff into cupboards and testing the essential oil diffuser is happening soon." Her fingertip bounced off the screen again. "Mattress delivery scheduled for tomorrow. Couch is arriving Wednesday. Everything is under control."

"All right." He didn't buy her rainbows-and-unicorns act but wouldn't pressure her to reveal more. Not at this early juncture of his visit.

Teacup peered out the windshield like an engineer conducting an old-fashioned train, golden ears perking and hairbow bobbling. The animal yipped, and Janie soothed the dog.

"How did this little one do last night?" she asked Keon, glancing at him for the briefest of moments. His chest tightened. Would it kill her to meet his gaze for more than a split-second? She angled her head and addressed the animal. "Were you a good girl?"

Teacup whined, lifting a paw from the security of her harness in the regulation booster seat.

Keon permitted himself a smile at Janie's interaction with the Yorkie. It seemed she intended to use the dog as an emotional shield for the rest of the day. Maybe he had to accept that. Chatting about the dog might act as an icebreaker of sorts, moving them past this unwelcome awkwardness.

"She plastered herself against my back on the sofabed all night," he replied. "I felt like I was wearing a teddy bear."

Janie's mouth curved. "She's spoiled."

"Like Tania?" Keon teased. His phone instructed him to continue through an intersection and take the next left. "Do these directions sound correct?" he asked, sensing a sudden chill in the air.

Janie bit her bottom lip. "I think so. Today is my first time going to Tania and Trey's new place. I'll text her if we get lost." She tugged in a breath. "Tania isn't spoiled," she said in a testy tone. "She's stressed." Head turning, she gazed out the passenger window.

Keon cursed his stupidity. As easy as snapping his fingers, he'd said something dense, offending his ex.

Hands sliding on the steering wheel, he negotiated the Rosevale streets. Cute shops and treed boulevards gave way to a residential area featuring new-looking townhouses, high-end condo complexes, and older bungalows.

"Tania is having a hard time," he said. "I shouldn't have joked about it. I'm sorry." Tania Hoyt was a great person, and, as Trey's fiancée, also Keon's friend of a few years. Her parents had split when she was little, and family relationships were strained.

He needed to learn when to keep his mouth shut. Neither he nor Janie knew what it felt like to grow up without both parents. Janie was tight with her twin brother and their parents, and Keon had a close-knit family back home.

Changing lanes, he swept a look across the console. "Janie, I realize you might feel uncomfortable working with me on wedding stuff. I'll try not to be a pest." For example, right now, regardless of the urge building inside him, he wouldn't blurt out how beautiful she looked in her lacy short-sleeved top and lightweight summer pants the same gray-blue shade as her skies-before-a-rain eyes.

Neither would he mention that, while they'd shopped for non-perishables for the condo, he'd daydreamed about them browsing a wholesale club back home. As a couple. He wouldn't utter a word about the fantasy of helping her choose towel colors and kitchen chairs and maybe selecting a leash and collar and bulk freezer portions of healthy raw dog food for the border collie or springer spaniel playing in their large, fenced yard behind his family's garden center.

He might be slow as a pot of simmering soup, but it was finally dawning on him that Janie hadn't cut him out of her life to hurt him. No, she'd ended contact to *protect* herself. Her comments at the flower shop had hinted as much.

Which meant...a weight in his chest lifted...she might have unwittingly fallen too deep, like he had.

Or was he getting ahead of himself?

"Okay," she finally responded, looking at him again. "But are you up for this? It's a lot of work."

The condo prep or fighting their attraction? He lifted a shoulder. "I didn't come to Rosevale early to sit on my ass." He forced his attention on the road, but it was hard faking disinterest in this woman—whom he'd pined over and thought about for a year—seated one tiny lap dog away.

Three hours ago, when he'd entered the backroom of Sunshine & Roses, his heart had ached at the sight of her. *Janie*. His friend for ten months, and then, for the remaining eight weeks of his year in Washington, his girlfriend and passionate lover.

Janie, the quirky weed-whacking florist.

The woman who'd taken the practice of deadheading flowers to a whole new level.

Who had probably pictured *his* head on the green stems of the colorful blossoms they'd planted.

The only woman who'd inspired him to consider a for-the-rest-of-his-life relationship. Just *her*.

Just Janie.

If these feelings were love, there was no escaping them. For him. But was it fair—to her—to do anything about it? To pursue her?

He suspected *not*.

Not when an international border and close family ties on both their parts separated them.

"Like I said this morning, I'm here to help with the wedding, and that's it," he said. Well, that was it *now*. Yesterday, while boarding the plane in BC, he'd entertained different ideas. "If you're okay with it, we're apartment-prep partners."

She inhaled. "Like coworkers?"

He tilted his head. He liked 'partners.' But he wouldn't argue. He craved peace between them.

"Coworking partners," he said by way of compromise. An eye on traffic, he extended his hand across the console, below Teacup's nose. The dog wormed backward on the booster seat. "Shake on it?"

Janie's lips pressed together. Her hand zigzagged over to meet his, her fingers small and delicate. They completed a quick shake, and a bolt of heat shot up his arm. Keon focused on driving.

The automated phone voice delivered a last command: *"You have arrived at your destination."*

But he was nowhere near *his* destination—a future with Janie. She needed to want it as badly as he did.

Otherwise, he was just spinning his wheels.

Inside Tania and Trey's empty two-bedroom condo, Janie took advantage of Keon's latest trek to the truck to pull her brother's paper-napkin advice out of her bra. She reread the note—*Opportunity knocks. Deal with your crap*—before transferring the napkin to her purse. That chore out of the way, she retrieved the replacement essential oil diffuser exchanged at the wholesale club on Tania's behalf. Her friend had said to operate the diffuser for twenty minutes. The original had caved at five. Properly functioning devices released scent for hours.

She ran tap water into the unit and unwrapped a vial from the packaging. At the granite-topped breakfast bar, she glanced over her shoulder to check on Teacup snoozing on a pet bed below the bowed living room windows, paws spreadeagled.

Janie's lips pulled into a smile, and a wave akin to longing flowed through her. Her mom often reminisced that when Janie and Derek were toddlers, they could be forgiven for almost any mischievous behavior once they were asleep. Evidently, that was when they were at their most adorable. Watching Teacup—and imagining an adorable napping baby instead...Tania and Trey's infant, not hers,—Janie understood her mom's logic.

"Teacup," she whispered. "Wait until a tiny Whitaker comes along. You'll need to change your princessy ways." Janie returned her attention to the diffuser. Some oils were toxic to dogs and cats, but lavender was harmless. Still, Janie doubted she'd use them around an infant. Why take a chance? If this were her new place, or her and Keon's place, if they lived together—

She gave her head a firm shake. *Stop thinking about living with Keon.* Or the next thing she knew, she'd be fantasizing about *their* baby and not Tania and Trey's. That way lay disaster for her peace of mind. Besides, if Tania and Trey weren't tying the knot, Janie's brain wouldn't have latched onto babies or sharing this gleaming apartment with Keon. It wasn't her taste anyway. Weddings simply made people nuts.

She sprinkled in several drops of lavender oil, plugged in the diffuser, and turned it on. A fine mist filtered into the air, releasing a soothing aroma.

Stepping around the breakfast bar, she located the sole drinking glass in the Shaker cabinets, washed it with a squirt of dish soap, and filled the tumbler with cool water.

Breathing in the calming lavender scent, she turned and nearly slammed into her ex.

"Keon! Oh, my God." Her heart bashed her ribs

as the water sloshed but didn't spill. "Why on earth are you looming behind me?" The pounding in her chest intensifying, she retreated to the living room side of the breakfast bar and set down the glass.

His hands lifted, palms out. "I'm not looming. I just came in." His tongue swiping over his delectable lips, he gazed at the glass. "Cold water sounds good."

"Help yourself," Janie replied, pushing the glass across the counter. "FYI, it's the only glass here and I don't know where it came from. I've already used it, so rinse it out. The tap works." Her heart skipped an annoying beat. As hot as he was—and by that she meant extremely attractive—Keon Rivers could dry up, well, a *river* with his hotness.

A corner of his mouth crooked upward. "Nah. This is fine." And then...his kissable lips imprinted on the rim where hers had been.

She caught hold of the counter to steady her balance as she watched him swallow. Memories of their eight weeks as a couple assailed her. Of holding hands last July as they'd strolled the Seattle waterfront, the summer sun beaming down upon them. Enjoying wine indoors on rainy June evenings as they'd shared their days and discussed friends, families, and career paths in an effort—on her part anyway—not to zero in on the powerful emotions that had quickly developed.

Allowing him to lend a hand with the apartment preparations endangered her equilibrium. Oh, did it ever.

More recollections traveled from deep within her consciousness to batter her tender heart. Visions of choosing blossoms with her cuddly Canadian cutie for the garden they'd cultivated on her building's raised beds. Making love in *her* bed afterward. Kissing and connecting. Feeling like she'd found her perfect match.

Except that had been a fantasy. Or was she wrong?

Stepping toward her, he set down the glass before gesturing toward several moving boxes stacked near a closed bedroom door. "Wasn't Heath here Saturday, hauling in cartons of clothes to hang in closets?" he asked.

"Yeah, why?"

"The glass."

"Of course," Janie remarked as her gray matter sparked to life. She pointed at the tumbler on the counter. "That must be Heath's." Although why the groom's younger brother would bring a drinking glass into the condo instead of a reusable sports bottle was odd.

"Which means—" Keon moved closer. Too close. Like, within six inches. "—we can share." His grin flashed, revealing even white teeth. His arm swung around her waist. He grabbed the glass and drank again.

"Keon," she sputtered. "What if I have—"

"A cold?" He shook his head. "No symptoms that I can tell." He peered at her lips. "Foot-in-mouth disease? A possibility."

Janie set her shoulders. "I do not have foot-in-mouth disease." Determined to prove she didn't fear his cute Canadian cooties, she extracted the glass from his fingers, placed the edge to her lips, and sipped.

Where his lips had touched. Over *her* previously applied lip prints. Her upper lip tingled. Her lower lip joined in on the action. The cool liquid crept down her throat.

She placed the half-empty glass on the breakfast bar.

Keon's eyebrows cocked like an outlaw in an Old West saloon. The visual had never appealed to her—until this instant.

"Hmm," he uttered, all gravel. Most outlawish.

He picked up the glass. Watching Janie, he drank a third time. Then paused, his dark brown gaze assessing.

She snorted. "Now what?"

Wiping his hand across his mouth, he held out the glass. She glanced at the contents. A few ounces remained.

"Drink," he whispered. "To the last drop."

A shiver wove through her...upper abdomen. His husky voice made their Duel of the Water Glass sound deliciously dirty.

A *good* sort of dirty.

Good, clean, dirty fun.

Like kisses and snuggles and the mornings beneath the sheets she remembered.

She marshaled her defenses. She didn't have the stomach for good or clean and especially not dirty fun. Emotionally, she wouldn't survive.

Channeling an Old West barmaid who refused to tolerate any flak, she snatched the glass, stared her ex-boyfriend in his sensual brown eyes, and poured the remaining water down the sink.

A sexy frown curved his mouth. He stepped even closer. "It's empty."

"Yep." Like her romantic future.

"We could fill it up again."

She shook her head. "I'm satisfied." Not by a long shot. But the truth of *that* matter was best kept to herself.

His foot edged around hers on the high-end laminate hardwood. Janie sidestepped him, blocking access to the glass and sink.

He gazed at her, black eyebrows wiggling.

Her heart bopped around inside her chest. Damn it, he was trying to distract her.

His arm looped around her waist. He grabbed for the glass but missed. His fingertips caught on the diffuser cord, and the device crashed onto the floor, popping open. Lavender-scented liquid splattered at their feet.

Swearing, Keon scooped up the top and bottom pieces. "Did we break it?" Gaze serious, he examined the lower half.

"*We?*" Janie glanced over at Teacup. The Yorkie's nostrils twitched. Teacup's tiny head lifted, but the dog only yawned before repositioning herself on her bed.

"Janie," Keon said from somewhere behind her. "Here are paper towels. If we work together, we'll have the mess cleaned in a flash."

She swung her head back around. As quick on

his feet as an invisible man, he'd set the diffuser on the breakfast bar and busted a roll out of the eighteen-pack he must have placed...somewhere. Last she'd known, the package had sat in the hall outside the apartment, along with several others.

He shoved a wad of paper towels into her hand, dampened a mass at the sink, and dropped to the floor with fistfuls of wet and dry. Fragrant water soaking his knees, he sopped up the mess.

"Careful," he warned as his hand slipped to hit the base of the breakfast bar. "The oil makes the water slippery."

Janie lowered to her knees beside him. Avoiding drenching her pants—and grateful the smell of lavender masked Keon's captivating Canadian-woods scent—she said, "Tania doesn't need to hear about this."

"Agreed." He scrubbed the floor.

"Let's just deal with it. If we broke the diffuser and need to buy another, we will. In fact, we should pick up a new unit regardless. I'll pay for this one and give her the next."

Continuing to clean, he nodded.

"We're lucky we didn't knock the glass off the counter." Janie stood and tossed the saturated paper towels into the sink. Keon lobbed her a messy handful. She caught his portion, pitched it onto the first batch, tore more sheets off the roll, and passed him several. "That glass could've broken into a trillion shards," she said as they toiled. "Teacup might have stepped on a sharp piece, slicing her paws into ribbons."

Keon raked his fingers through the thick ebony hair flopping onto his forehead. "I'm way ahead of you. Anything that happens this week is between us."

"You're damn right it is." Janie had committed to creating an anxiety-free environment for the bride, and she wasn't about to fall short her first day on the job. "What happens in Tania's condo *stays* in Tania's condo." That sounded less couple-like than the way he'd said it.

He cleaned the last of the mess. "I'll find garbage bags." He got up and pivoted toward the hall. "We can't leave half a roll of used paper towels drying in the sink."

Janie looked over the breakfast island to the cabinets and counters. The wads overflowed one side of the classy black tub.

"We might have overreacted to the situation," she said to her ex's retreating form. *She'd* overreacted. Even so, they had worked well together. Like the wedding-disaster prevention team they were supposed to be.

And she hadn't experienced the impulse to kiss him once.

Liar, she thought, cheeks warming.

Chapter Five

Keon hustled toward the foyer of the bride and groom's formerly spotless new condo, on a mission to retrieve the garbage bags. He shouldn't have messed around with Janie and the water glass. He'd wanted to remind her of their many light-hearted moments as a couple, not create a hazard for Teacup. Time was short, considering they needed to organize Trey and Tania's belongings before Friday. The bride had earmarked the hours before the rehearsal dinner as a bridesmaid spa day, and Heath had arranged a round of golf for the guys.

Rounding the corner, he muttered a curse. The door had caught on the eighteen-pack of paper towels he'd brought in from the hall, creating a wedge of space large enough to accommodate a curious Yorkie.

Hauling in the package, he poked his head into the seventh-floor corridor. The harmonious notes of South Asian flute music issued quietly from an apartment across the passage and two doors down. But if he strained his ears, was that the elevator doors whisking open or closed?

He couldn't see the recessed elevator bank from here, only the neighboring doors and the open cardboard boxes overflowing with kitchen and bathroom items. No one—not a human being, not a cat, not a tiny dog, probably not even an ant—occupied the common area.

He yanked his head back into the foyer. "Janie," he called over his shoulder, propping open the door with a runner-clad foot. "Is Teacup still asleep?" Dreading the answer, he held his breath.

"No." Janie appeared around the corner. "Is she with you?" Eyes huge, she glanced around. "Keon?"

His stomach bottomed out. "Check the bedrooms and the bathrooms." He raced into the hall. "And the closets. And the sunroom."

"What happened?" She hurried to the front door.

"The paper towels." He glanced down the

passage in both directions. Nothing. No one. "I blew it, bringing them in. Teacup might've gotten out."

"*Out?* Where?"

He flapped a hand. "Search the condo. I'll check the elevator." He headed into the hallway.

"*The elevator?*" She began following him.

"Janie!"

She ran back inside. Keon rushed to the elevator. As he reached the steel doors, Janie bolted back into the hall.

"The doors to the bedrooms are closed," she shouted.

He banged the elevator button. "Did you search them? How about the bathrooms?"

"No." She dashed across the hall and rapped on a neighbor's door. "She was sleeping in the living room. She can't open doors."

Keon glanced at the elevator lights. "It's going down." They were on the top floor. The dog couldn't have traveled higher. He hoped. "Is there a roof area? Like at your building?"

She shook her head, sandy-blond hair swinging. "That's why Tania and Trey chose a unit with a sunroom."

He nodded. "I'll take the stairs. You stay here. In

case Teacup got into the elevator with someone and they check her tags and bring her back."

"Keon, hurry!" She pounded on a second door in the hall. "Check every floor. She could be in the lobby. In the underground parking. Or outside. Tania will kill us."

Keon whipped open the heavy stairwell door and bounded down the stairs as a neighbor answered Janie's frantic knocking.

"What's going on?" a deep voice boomed.

"We lost a dog." This from Janie.

The pounding of his feet echoed off the walls as he grabbed the cool handrail and hopped to the next landing. The bewilderment and worry on Janie's face filled him. *His* fun and games were responsible.

Janie was right. If he didn't find Teacup—safe, without one golden hair out of place—Tania would kill him. First, though, Trey would strangle him. Heath would knock him out cold. And Janie would never speak to him again. He would never return home.

Unless by body bag.

"You haven't seen her?" Janie pleaded with the across-the-hall neighbor. "Yea big." She hovered one palm over the other, showing about eight inches. "Five pounds. Her name is Teacup."

The middle-aged man shook his head. "Sorry. I haven't." He cleared his throat. "My name is Hugh." He held out his hand, and Janie stared at his blunt-tipped fingers, realizing too late that he was being polite. "You are?" he asked.

"Janie." Instructing herself to calm down, she shook his hand. Her legs twitched with the urge to hurtle down the stairwell after Keon. If she intercepted him with a text, she could search floors six and five, leaving him to scout the lobby and other areas she'd rather not think about. Like underground parking. A scary place for a toy breed. Where sedans, crossovers, vans, and dangerous trucks lurked.

Upon their arrival at the four-building complex, Janie had spotted not only small pickups in the subterranean cavern but also hulking Dodges, Chevys, and Fords. Complete with mud flaps, acres of shiny chrome, and engines evoking formidable images of scaly dragons roaring to life.

At any moment, one of those vehicles might barrel out of its space. The garage door would yawn agape, and a frightened Yorkie could scamper into the burnished light of late afternoon in an anxiety-fueled attempt to track down her human-parents.

Then there was the busy street and intersection. People jogging, walking, strolling. Vehicles honking. Tires squealing. Animal-kickers. Dognappers!

Pasting on a courteous smile, she presented a calm veneer. Panicking wouldn't help. Keon was on the case, and she trusted him.

"That's rough about your Yorkie," Hugh said. "Apologies if I sounded rude when you knocked. I thought you were that kid from three."

"That's okay." She *had* pummeled Hugh's door like a Norse god brandishing a hammer. "What kid from three?"

The music in the next condo quieted. Two mid-thirties women in yoga gear emerged.

"Did someone knock?" the shorter woman with tawny curls asked. "We were meditating."

Her companion—taller and curvier, with warm brown skin—smiled. "Then we heard Hugh's voice."

Hugh gestured toward Janie. "Mariah, Natalie, this is Janie. She lost her dog."

"The door was open a crack," Janie explained after shaking hands with the newcomers. Keon had said he'd messed up. Which must mean either he'd left the door open when he'd fetched the paper towels, or it hadn't fully shut behind him. Janie would bet her job at Sunshine & Roses on the latter. Keon Rivers was a great guy. Helpful. Supportive. He wouldn't intentionally place an innocent animal in danger. "Just a crack," she repeated, feeling compelled to defend him even though neither woman batted an eyelash.

Another door opened. A man and woman in their late fifties or early sixties ventured into the hall. Both wore wedding rings.

"What's up?" the man asked as Janie cast a worried glance toward the elevator.

"Janie in 708 lost her dog," Hugh said.

The woman's eyes widened. "The newlyweds!" She swooped to Janie's side and clasped her hand. "I'm Madge. I love weddings." She examined Janie's left fingers. "No ring?"

Janie extricated her hand. Not that it was any of Madge's business, but she replied, "We're not the newlyweds. The couple—Tania and Trey—are getting married this weekend. My—my—*friend* and I are moving them in." With a palm to her chest, she composed her breathing. *Friends*. All right. She could work with that. More to the point, she needed to. Now that she'd let Keon back into her life, she didn't know if she could bear booting him out a second time. They had too much—uh, too many acquaintances in common. Likely, more weddings requiring their *individual* attendances lurked in their *separate* futures.

Madge smiled as she returned to the side of the man Janie assumed was her husband. "What a nice gift idea," the woman said, "moving in the newlyweds. But why bring your dog?"

"She's not ours. She's Tania and Trey's. We're dog-sitting." Janie shot another troubled look toward the elevator. Whatever had compelled her to knock on so many doors? Where was Keon? Why hadn't he called or texted?

She curled her fingers around the phone in her pants pocket. Should she interrupt him at what might be a precarious moment? She retrieved the device.

The man with Madge frowned. "I got home five minutes ago. I didn't see a dog."

"But were you *looking*?" Madge prodded.

"I guess not."

Natalie stepped closer. "There's an eight-year-old on the third floor who punches the elevator buttons. I hope your friend's dog didn't run inside."

Janie winced. "Me too." This situation sounded

worse and worse! But Teacup couldn't have just disappeared.

Chewing her lip, she tapped a text to Keon:

Any luck?

No gray dot bubbles popped up on her screen.

Her stomach knotted. She couldn't wait one more second. "Thank you, everyone, but I'm gonna—"

"Wait." Madge clutched her forearm. "The elevator light came on."

Natalie crossed her fingers. "Here's hoping that's your man. With the sweet pup."

Peeling off Madge's excited grip, Janie dashed to the elevator, a lump in her throat.

Everyone followed.

The doors swished open. Keon stood inside, cradling a bewildered-looking Teacup, a serious expression on his handsome face and portions of his black hair sticking up, as if he'd raked his fingers through the sexy mop during his search.

Janie could have wept with relief. "Keon! Thank you."

His gaze drifted over her cobbled-together support squad. Looking at her, he nodded.

"Ma'am." He deposited the wriggling dog into her hands.

Teacup licked her chin. The neighbors chuckled and oohed and applauded as Janie cuddled the squirming Yorkie against her beating heart.

"How gallant," Madge whispered, gazing at Keon.

Janie agreed. Whether it was the combination of his bedhead hair along with his form-fitting dark jeans and T-shirt or his aura of sincerity and damn sexy social responsibility, he looked like Batman surfacing from his underground crime lab.

He'd saved Teacup from real or imaginary bad guys, for sure.

She introduced him to the group. Natalie and Mariah offered their best wishes and promises to keep an eye out for Teacup's escapist tendencies once Tania and Trey returned from their honeymoon.

"Thanks," Keon called as the women disappeared into their condo. "Thanks to all of you," he said to the remaining three neighbors. "Sorry for the commotion. We're okay now." Gaze on Janie, he motioned her toward the open door of 708.

"You know," Madge said, tickling Teacup's scalp as Janie and Keon walked past, "as darling as this girl is, she's not permitted to run in the halls. It's against strata rules. *Carry* her to the elevator next time."

Hugh spread his palms. "Never mind quoting regulations for a first infraction, Madge. Now that we're acquainted, it's too bad you two"—he pointed at Keon and Janie—"aren't the folks moving in."

Janie laughed politely, but a flare of uneasiness burst inside her. In a series of unsettling images, she pictured herself and Keon finding a place together. Paging through real estate listings. Attending viewings. Preferably for a cozy starter home, not a bylaw-infested condo.

How implausible was that?

She had her work cut out for her during the remainder of his visit. Some way, somehow, she needed to continue providing Tania with a problem-free move-in from this point forward, while battling the rapid melting of the block of ice regarding Keon, which, over the past year, had protected her heart.

"We need to talk about this," Keon said as Janie carried Teacup inside the condo. Hyper-aware of the animal's misadventure, he peeled an ear for the clicking of the door tumblers before releasing the handle. "It's one thing not to tell Trey and Tania about the diffuser, but they need to know their dog got out. Worse, that she found her way *into* the elevator with no one noticing." Without him or Janie realizing the dog had awoken. He was supposed to help his ex-girlfriend ease the bride's stress, not stress *her* out instead.

He needed to reestablish his priorities. Continue moving in the engaged couple, perform his groomsman duties, then fly home, not play games intended to reignite Janie's interest, no matter the yearning pulling at him. Believing he could somehow convince her they were meant for each other was a pipe dream. *She* might be the woman for him, but her life was here. And he had responsibilities back home.

"What if the dog escapes again once Trey and Tania move in?" he asked, trailing woman and pup into the living room.

Teacup wriggled in her arms, and the dog's front paws scrambled his direction. Warmth suffused his chest as he recalled Teacup's cute hairdo tickling his chin while they rode the elevator to the seventh floor. But when the doors opened and he'd spotted

Janie, the gratitude in *her* eyes had heated him through.

She restrained the Yorkie's movements. "I know," she responded, resignation threading her tone. "I don't want to admit that I—we—let Teacup out of sight. But if we don't tell Tania, a neighbor will. Like Madge."

"Then we're on the same page?"

"Yes. On one condition. Tania finds out *after* the honeymoon."

The rubber band in Keon's chest constricted. He hated that his carelessness with the paper towels had influenced Janie to hide the truth from one of her closest friends.

Her hand popped up, curtailing further debate. "I don't want Tania worrying about her fur-baby when she and Trey should celebrate their love." Snuggling Teacup tight, she kissed the Yorkie's ears. Keon felt insanely jealous of the tiny dog.

He rubbed his chin. "Has Tania mentioned Teacup running out of their old place?"

"Not since they first adopted her. When they take her outside, they use a leash as well as carrying her to the elevator, as per building rules for a dog this size. Teacup loves Trey, but this girl sticks like glue to Tania."

"And neither of us is Tania." Keon glanced over his shoulder at the boxes in the foyer and then at the stack waiting to be unpacked outside the primary bedroom. Several containers from the wholesale club remained in the common corridor. He would haul the lot inside before driving Janie home and returning Teacup to Heath's for the night. Tomorrow, fresh and rested, they could begin unpacking.

He chucked the dog under the chin. "Who's looking after this little devil during the honeymoon?"

Horror dawned in Janie's eyes. "Oh, no. Tania must have considered that. Until the Mr. Sprinkles incident, Teacup was supposed to stay with Mrs. Hoyt."

"Maybe one sister can stay here instead, with Teacup."

"Or spot each other off, giving Teacup a chance to get used to her new home. Failing that, maybe she can stay longer at Heath's?"

"I'm not sure. It's nice he can help this week, but he has a bit of a social life." That was an understatement.

Janie grinned. "You noticed? Well, I'll take her," she pronounced with a firm nod. "I'll check with Roslyn about keeping her in the back of Sunshine &

Roses while I'm working. Or maybe that's when Tami and Noni can pitch in. Between those two, myself, and Heath, we'll manage." Jiggling the dog against her hip, Janie asked the animal, "How about it, sweetie? Want to sleep at Auntie Janie's for a couple of weeks?"

Yes. The thought jet-planed into Keon's mind. *I do.*

But she wasn't asking him.

"She needs to bond with me," Janie said. "Then everything will work out."

Teacup whimpered, squirming in her arms.

"What's wrong?" she asked the animal in an earnest voice. "Do you need to pee?"

"She can't already," Keon said. "She just went."

"Went? Where?"

"In the lobby." He stepped closer to the captivating duo.

"The *lobby*?" Janie echoed as the dog scrabbled free of her hold and launched her tiny body toward Keon. "Here she comes!"

He caught the pup, smiling when T-Dog licked his stubble.

Janie snorted. "This is rich. I cart her around like royalty, but she dotes on the alpha." Her nose crinkled. "Who smells like a lavender field, I might add."

He laughed. The lingering scent of essential-oil-laced water carried from the damp patches at his knees. "I was there when she needed me. She's grateful."

"For saving her. Like a princess in a fairy tale. Was she in the lobby when you found her?"

He nodded. "I caught up to her after she whizzed on some flyers on the floor by the mailboxes. She was sitting there like a tiny sphinx."

"Oh, boy. Well, it's good it seems she's kind of well-behaved. What if someone had opened the lobby door and she'd gone outside?"

"I doubt she put much thought into it. Trey told me she was trained to use papers and puppy pads." As well as replaceable live-grass patches, a dog's version of a litter box. Trey had provided Heath a patch to use at his place and in the condo sunroom. "I'll bring the indoor grass tomorrow." Keon should have anticipated needing the box today.

"Great idea," Janie replied. "But I feel awful. We should have walked her before driving over here. Her bladder is the size of a marshmallow. I *know* that. What kind of friend am I?"

Not any worse a friend than him.

"Don't beat yourself up about it. She had plenty of opportunities to use the box at Heath's." The dog's head bobbed as Teacup's attention flew back and forth between himself and Janie. "After I found her, I dug her leash out of the truck and walked her to the pet park for the complex. She did number two and another squirt of one. The good news is, she *didn't* go on Trey and Tania's new floors."

"Then she's relieved?" Janie asked, stroking the dog's cowpoke mustache.

"She is completely and totally relieved."

Head lowering, Janie went nose-to-muzzle with the dog. "You're relieved, and *I'm* relieved. I think it's fair to say Keon is relieved." She patted the spot behind Teacup's wilted hairbow.

"I definitely am." Not only because Teacup was safe. In these last few moments, it felt like the invisible barrier between him and Janie had begun a slow descent. Hopefully, the next few days would create room for something new to blossom. Which meant Teacup's efforts to empty her miniature bladder had wound up in his favor.

And, for that, he was *greatly* relieved.

Chapter Six

AT FIVE THE NEXT MORNING, Keon woke from dreams of snuggling Janie as his phone blasted a cheery refrain from the living room side table in Heath's apartment. T-Dog—and not Janie, unfortunately—slept in a warm ball against his naked chest. Reaching over the sofa arm, he silenced the alarm that had cut short his satisfying dreams and kicked off the blanket bunched over his boxer shorts.

"Teacup," he whispered, imagining murmuring sweet words to Janie instead. He scratched the dog's ears as he planted the soles of his feet on cool hardwood. "Wakey-wakey. Shake a tail."

The Yorkie yawned and squirmed. Leaning forward, Keon placed the pint-sized animal on the floor. Barking, she trotted to the rectangular box of live grass in front of the sundeck window, sniffed the patch, and turned in three circles.

As if daring him to look away, the dog stared at him and blinked. She squatted to squirt number one and followed that up with a tidy pile of two. She loped to her water bowl beside the dinette table and lapped, her stinky business forgotten.

Keon tipped his head. "Huh." Being a princess had its perks. Standing, he headed for the box of compostable dog bags on the kitchen counter.

Heath sauntered out of his bedroom in bare feet and PJ pants. Glancing at Keon, he gagged and waved his hand in front of his nose. "Dude. You reek."

"It's not me. It's the dog." Keon started the elaborate coffee machine his friend loaded with locally roasted beans every night. As the grinder whirred, he retrieved a bag. "It's not that bad."

Heath smirked. "Yeah, yeah. *Dude*. You snuck one in there."

"It's not *me*," Keon repeated. "It's the dog."

"So you say." Heath wriggled his fingers. "Gimme the bag. I can't let you take all the credit for looking after the beast. How will she love me after you move to the hotel?"

In two more nights. Keon snorted. "Have it your

way," he said as the grinding faded. The machine shifted into brewing mode. "I'm taking a run and grabbing a shower." The rich aroma of dark roast filled the air. He looked forward to enjoying a mug post-workout.

"And then you're going to Janie's?" Heath asked, making faces as he plugged his nose and cleaned Teacup's mess.

"Yeah. After I catch up on some work." Keon had brought his laptop for the purpose. He'd rather head straight to Janie's, but business called.

Heath tied off the bag. "Drop this into the outside garbage on your way." He lobbed the bag into the air.

Stepping back, Keon spread his arms. The bag plopped onto the floor. "Put it nicely"—he pointed at the sack—"beside the door, and I will."

Heath twirled a finger at Teacup and then the bag. "Girl. Go get your stuff."

The dog danced on her hind legs and barked.

"Good girl," Heath praised the animal. "Who *wants* to carry poop?" He took the sack to the entry.

Keon scoffed. "You thought she'd carry it for you?"

"It was worth a try." Bending, Heath stroked the dog's head as she pranced. "But she's smarter than she looks." He wet a paper towel at the kitchen sink.

"That's what no one says about you."

Heath didn't take the bait. "I thought your mom was covering for you at the garden center." He returned to the living room and dabbed at spots on the grass patch as Teacup yapped, supervising.

Keon retrieved his toothbrush and jogging gear from his duffel bag beside the couch. "Mom is lending a hand if necessary. But Hamaguchi's is my responsibility now. I want Mom and Dad to enjoy their early retirement." Stepping into his running shorts, he poked his chin toward the grass box. "You know, you do that so carefully it's like you're wiping a baby's bottom."

Unfazed, Heath disposed of the paper towel. "I plan on fully taking part in the parenting process when my time comes." He washed and dried his hands.

Keon located his running shoes. "Oh?" Heath hadn't mentioned becoming serious with a woman before, much less having a kid. "When might that happen?" Surely not before Keon fathered a child. Although the only woman he'd ever imagined sharing parenting duties with was Janie.

"From where I sit," Heath said, "maybe sooner

than you. Unless you have plans with someone back home, Antarctica will shrink and grow a tropical forest before you get your ass in gear with Janie." Heath, the mind reader, poured himself a cup of steaming coffee. "In the meantime, her attention might wander. I'm surprised it hasn't already." Heath gave a lopsided grin. "Maybe it'll slide on over to sweet Heath." He snickered.

Keon narrowed his gaze. His friend wouldn't dare hit on Janie. "Why'd you say that?" He pulled on a moss-green *Hamaguchi's Fruit and Garden Centre* T-shirt. Sitting on the couch, he reached for his socks. Teacup romped over and chewed a shoelace.

Heath flourished a hand up and down his six-pack abs. "Isn't it obvious?"

"Stop breaking my balls about Janie, man." Keon pushed a foot into a runner.

"Kee. *Buddy*. My clerk busting her wrist is a bonus for you. Without that little twist of fate, *I'd* be helping your dream girl with the condo stuff." He sipped his coffee. "You know what they say about male pheromones and proximity."

Keon laughed. "You read *Cosmo* now?"

"I page through when I'm around a copy, yeah. I'm not a cave dweller. Dude, everyone knows

Janie is your dream girl. You might as well admit it."

Keon wrestled his second runner away from a playfully snarling Teacup. "If I admit it to her, she'll run scared."

"What can I tell you?" Heath swaggered toward the bedroom with his coffee. Teacup's head popped up, and she trotted over to join Heath. At the door, Heath looked back. "I realize you don't have my looks and pull with the ladies, but nothing ventured, nothing gained." He grinned like the demon he was. "Am I wrong?"

After his run, Keon hopped in the shower, his conversation with Heath chomping into the corners of his mind like a video-game character gobbling points. Thoughts pelted him from all directions as he washed his body and hair, the hot water rushing over his upturned face. Last Sunday, when he'd boarded the plane in Kelowna, his mission had seemed clear. See Janie again, spend time together, and determine if he was in love with the woman.

He hadn't truly considered the ramifications of his choices, which was unlike him. That was, if he didn't count falling into bed with Janie one passionate spring night last year. His big head hadn't been screwed on properly then, either. How could he not have foreseen that getting intimate with the woman would cause trouble? His attraction to her had overwhelmed him, but now he realized his *feelings* had been the driving force.

From the start, he'd felt drawn to Janie. Sometimes, during a group event, he would catch her scoping him out. They'd flirted, but he'd restrained himself from taking things too far. Later, once they were dating, she'd said she'd experienced an instant sizzle too.

When they finally got together following an outdoor concert, they woke in bed eager to continue seeing each other, but under defined parameters designed to minimize heartache. As if that were possible, he realized now. But, back then, not getting in too deep seemed like the answer. No talking about messy lovey-dovey stuff. If either of them suspected they were developing feelings that would be difficult to rein in once he left Washington, they would end their arrangement.

Except he hadn't once broached the subject, even when he knew damn well that he was falling for her. Over those eight amazing weeks, Janie hadn't mentioned going goo-goo-eyed for him. Not when she made him a surprise candlelight dinner. Or checked out fruit-farming books from the library to learn more about the history of the business that had built the cornerstone of his immigrant grand-parents' lives. For Keon, the carefully constructed framework of their relationship had enabled him to push away or outright ignore signs he was stumbling, tumbling, and bumbling his way into a life-altering situation.

He stepped out of the shower and dried off to Teacup's plaintive whining outside the bathroom door. After he dressed, a quick inspection of the apartment confirmed Heath had left for work. By the time Keon fired up his laptop with another cup of coffee, the dog snoozing beneath the table at his feet, his concerns about how to move forward with Janie had swirled into a maelstrom.

Fingers striking the laptop keys, he dug into a spreadsheet. Last spring and summer, he had been dense as dirt to believe he could become temporarily involved with a woman as captivating, beautiful, and caring as Janie McAllister. Once home working on the Hamaguchi's expansion, he'd missed her with an intensity he hadn't realized was possible. Her infectious laugh and corny jokes. He'd tried talking himself out of his misery, turning his attention to business and family and exploring new relationships in an ultimately futile attempt to eradicate the staggering feeling that he'd accidentally fallen in love.

Because no matter how many women he'd dated, none of them were Janie. And now, after only a couple of days since his plane had touched down in the States, their bond was reigniting. The way her skin flushed when he was near told him as much. As did the connection that sizzled like sparks in the air when she cast him a sidelong glance.

Life would be so much easier if they'd never met. Rebooting their relationship would require one of them to make drastic changes. From what he'd noticed with friends back home, long-distance romances either fizzled or progressed.

He didn't want to start things up again with Janie only to experience another painful fizzle. He ached to progress.

Teacup woke and pawed his leg until he settled the tiny dog into a warm bundle on his lap. Two hours later, Keon shut the laptop and gathered supplies the princess might require throughout the day.

While driving to Janie's with the dog, he called

Trey. They decided Keon should purchase a second live-grass container to leave at the condo. Keon didn't bring up the question of dog care during the honeymoon. Tania wasn't the sort of person to let the matter slide. Plus, he wouldn't be around, so it wasn't his business.

He tightened his grip on the steering wheel, mulling over things. If he moved some pieces of his life around and volunteered to stay in Rosevale for another two weeks, why couldn't *he* look after the dog? Either at Heath's place, or at Janie's while she worked, or at Trey and Tania's new apartment.

Another fourteen days to get things right with his former—and perhaps future—girlfriend.

He tapped his fingertips on the steering wheel. Staying longer would affect the garden-center expansion. Summer was their busiest time, and every family member chipped in. But if Janie was the woman for him, he needed to prove to her that he was a guy worth taking a chance on.

Brooding, he pulled up to her building and texted his arrival. His mood brightened when she climbed into the truck wearing hip-hugging jeans and a bright blue T-shirt, a computer tablet tucked beneath one arm and a stylus pen stuffed into her untidy but adorably sexy bun. Folded printouts poked out of her open purse on the dirt-flecked floor mat.

He indicated the papers. "What are those?" He pictured her wielding the tablet like a clipboard while commanding the future floral department at Hamaguchi's. She suited the position perfectly. She suited *him* perfectly. But her life and family and friends were here.

"Furniture deliveries for today and tomorrow," she explained, fingers flicking toward the papers. Scrounging in her purse, she produced a canine dental stick. "Tania-approved." She held the treat below Teacup's twitching nose. The dog snatched the stick and settled on the regulation booster seat, the treat between her tiny paws. The animal gnawed.

As Keon maneuvered the truck out of the parking space, Janie's phone tumbled out of her purse onto the floor.

"Oops." She held up a hand, and he applied the brakes.

She retrieved the phone and shoved the device between the papers in her purse. Straightening, she repositioned the tablet on her lap. "Okay." Hands to her bun, she checked the stylus. "Ready."

He lifted his eyebrows. "You're sure about that?"

She squared her shoulders. "Yep. You know I like to be prepared."

Yes, he did. He steered the truck onto the street fronting her building.

She patted the cover of her tablet. "There's a lot to accomplish in a short time. It'll be easier keeping track of Tania's instructions on my tablet instead of my phone."

He sidled over another glance. The stylus in her bun wobbled. "You're not worried you'll lose the hair jewelry?"

She shook her head, and a tendril drifted free of her bun, brushing her cheek. His fingertips tingled with the impulse to trace its path. As if the strand itched her skin, she pushed the lock behind her ear and scratched her cheek. "It's no different from stabbing a pencil in there," she said.

"An *expensive* pencil."

"Not to worry, my Canadian cutie. I have everything under control."

Keon's tongue glued to the roof of his mouth, and he jerked his attention back to the traffic. Had she called him *her* Canadian cutie?

He hadn't heard those words in far too long. He yearned to hear them slip from her cotton-candy-pink lips every day.

She glanced over Teacup's bobbing head. "What I mean is, you're cute. And you're Canadian."

"But I'm not *your* Canadian cutie," he summed up with a forced smile.

Face rosy, she studied her fingernails. "I could use a latte."

"Got it." Deflated, he headed to the nearest coffeeshop.

Janie's face continued flaming as they visited a drive-through for lattes and croissants. She sipped her takeout cup while Keon parked at a luxury pet store and disappeared inside to buy a second live-grass patch for the sunroom in Tania and Trey's new condo.

"Teacup," she whispered to the dog, glancing out the windshield to double check his whereabouts. "I can't believe I called him my Canadian cutie. What was I thinking?" *Face it, Janie. Your feelings for him have never faded.*

The dog stopped chewing the treat, her head tipping and her brown eyes blinking.

"At least I didn't say my *cuddly* Canadian cutie." Janie stroked Teacup's soft ears. "Or my Canadian hottie." Both sweet nothings from when she and Keon dated. The 'cuddly' had started on a lazy weekend of Netflix and sleeping in, and the memories had her itching for her remote, Keon at her side. As for the 'hottie'—well, the thought had occurred practically every time he'd removed his shirt, and those memories *sizzled*. "Cuddly or hottie anything would have been a disaster." Unfortunately.

Ears pricking, Teacup stood up on the booster seat. Carrying the dental stick and stretching the harness strap, the animal hopped onto Janie's lap.

"No, girl. No." Grateful the tablet cover protected the electronic device from canine claws, Janie placed her latte in a cupholder. "I wasn't asking for cuddles from *you*. Or him." Although, Keon was a fantastic hugger. He hugged better than any man she knew, including her dad and brother. His hugs during chilly rainstorms were phenomenal. Definitely better than those of the guys she'd dated before he entered her life and shook it like a maraca.

But she shouldn't compare his hugs to those of men outside her gene pool. If she started down that treacherous path, she might compare his *kisses* to those of previous boyfriends. And trouble lurked around every corner of that road.

A dreamy sigh tumbled from her lips. Keon's

kisses were divine, his whisker stubble sexy without feeling rough, the movement of his mouth on hers tender and romantic, passionate and intense. Brimming with the longing he'd whispered to her more than once. Ripe with temptation.

Fantasizing about his amazing kisses might lead to memories of other intimate moments. Like his hands caressing her bare limbs. His body moving slowly above—or beneath—hers. The feeling of completion that had settled deep inside her whenever they'd made love.

The cold imprint of Teacup's nose pressed into her chin. Face scorching now, Janie shook her head.

Never mind not tiptoeing down Memory Lane! She'd sprinted into an arousing maze of reminiscing. And now, as she peered out the windshield, yes, *now* that every inch of her exposed skin tingled and heat gathered between her legs, the best boyfriend and lover of her life was strolling back toward the truck, purchases in hand.

She could not. *Believe*. Herself. She needed to muster some semblance of control.

Plucking Teacup off her lap, she returned the dog to the booster seat. "Teacup, stay. Chew." She stuck the gummy dental stick between the dog's paws.

Smiling, Keon opened the driver's door. "How's my girl?" He stuffed packages behind the seat.

"Great," Janie enthused, fanning her hot cheeks and hoping he didn't notice the erect state of her nipples beneath the fabric of her T-shirt. But, as she realized a moment later when he offered Teacup a new squeak toy, of course he'd meant the dog.

Well, she had answered on *behalf* of the dog. Not herself.

Sure, Janie. Keep telling yourself a bunch of fibs.

Chapter Seven

Not eager for a repeat of losing Teacup...or of more fantasies of Keon in a Wild West saloon...once inside the condo Janie suggested that one of them should always stay within sight of the pet. Relief flowed through her when Keon agreed. Following her humiliating gaffes in the truck, a certain tension had sprung up between them. Sort of like water boiling in a kettle forgotten on a stove. She could *feel* him thinking, but did she want him asking more questions, poking around in her messy emotions?

Her recommendation about the dog worked well. As Keon emptied dry goods into kitchen cabinets and she hung Tania's clothes in the primary bedroom's walk-in closet, Teacup pattered close on his heels. Not only that, but while waiting at her place this morning for Keon to pick her up, she'd checked with her boss about allowing Tania's dog into a gated space in the back of Sunshine & Roses. After receiving a thumbs-up from Roslyn, she called Tania to offer Yorkie honeymoon care, and the bride gushed her gratitude. Apparently, booking a last-minute pet hotel had proven more difficult than Tania or her mom had anticipated.

Janie hung the last of Tania's clothes. When she received a text signaling the arrival of the bedroom furniture, Keon settled Teacup in the sunroom, which Janie packed with the starfish, other toys, a full water dish, the remnants of the dental stick, three blankets, and the grass patch. She opened a screened window for fresh air and adjusted the blinds to welcome in a stream of sunshine.

After the bedroom furniture and mattresses were set up, she tipped the delivery guys and freed the dog from her sunny jail. The animal trailed her favored human—Keon—around the apartment.

Alone in the second bedroom, Janie kneeled on the high-end wood laminate and sliced open a small box marked **TANIA**. She extracted a silky negligee she recognized as one of Lacey DeMarco's elegant designs. Lacey had gifted the piece to Tania during her bachelorette party. Thanks to Janie's brilliant matchmaking capabilities, Lacey and Janie's brother became a couple that night.

Resting the lingerie on her lap, Janie stuffed her hand inside the box. Her fingers bumped a container too small for shampoo and too large for essential oil.

An instant later, she withdrew a bottle of—*ohhh*, sensual massage lotion.

She inspected the bottle. "This can't be right." She glanced around the intended guest bedroom, in her opinion a peculiar place in which to store intimate items.

She checked the list on her tablet. Tapping the stylus on the screen, she got up on her knees and scanned the room again.

"Keon," she said toward the open door. "Have you seen my phone? I need to call Tania." She set aside the tablet and stylus. Sitting on the floor with her legs folded to one side, she returned the items to the box.

Keon appeared in the doorway. Teacup sat at attention between his ankles.

"What's up?" Stepping inside, he handed Janie her phone. Teacup scampered alongside him as if an invisible rope connected the dog to the Favored One's jeans leg. "It was on the breakfast bar," the

Favored One said. *Her* Favored One as well as Teacup's. At another time, and in another life.

"Thanks." Janie shut the box flaps. "I think Tania and Trey meant to put this stuff in the primary bedroom. Except her instructions don't say where to store the, um, items."

The Favored One planted his hands on his hips. His canine adorer sniffed the box.

"What's in there?" Janie's former boyfriend asked.

"Nothing you need to know about." She shooed Teacup away from the box.

"Could Heath have put this box in here by mistake?" Keon asked in a thoughtful voice. "When he brought stuff from their old place?"

"I guess so." Hustle and bustle jam-packed these last days before the wedding. Errors were bound to occur. "I'll find out." Janie tapped her phone screen.

Crouching beside the box, Keon slid a finger beneath a cardboard flap. His tempting body heat radiated from his T-shirt-clad torso.

Janie slapped his hand. "Don't snoop."

He chuckled. "You snooped."

"I did not." She lifted her chin. "Tania's name is on the box."

"I can see that."

"The box is in this room."

"Agreed."

"I needed to open the box to determine if the items should be stored in this room. Or in the main bedroom. Or not in the apartment at all." She paused before tacking on, "Yet."

Grinning, Keon nudged the flap. "You're saying that whatever is in here would have shown up in the condo eventually? Although maybe not while we're here and might learn what's inside?"

Teacup whined, and Keon picked up the dog.

"Yes," Janie admitted, putting down her phone and brushing away a strand of hair that insisted on dangling from her bun.

Keon's eyebrows bobbed. "Might these items have anything to do with their, I don't know, love life?"

Ugh. Why must he continually try to get under her skin? "Ours is not to judge," she said with an indignant huff. "Ours is to organize."

"It's kind of hard not to judge when you make it sound like Trey is hiding a porn collection in there." He eyed the name on the box. "Or is it Tania's porn?"

"It's not porn!" As far as Janie knew. She hadn't snooped enough to find out. "But what should it matter to either of us if it is?"

"You're right," he responded solemnly. "Ours is not to judge. A few sex tapes never hurt anyone. Other than several celebrities. And my cousin—"

"*Keon.*"

"Hush." He covered Teacup's ears. "Not so loud."

"Not"—Janie snapped her fingers in front of his nose—"so annoying."

"You know me. I can't help myself. Look at it this way. Tania and Trey don't seem to need the porn now, or it wouldn't be in the box. Who knows? Maybe this is the box they always hide it in. And they haven't packed the porn in their suitcases for the honeymoon. So, I guess this stuff is for once they're back home. In case their spark dies somewhere down the road," he added with a chuckle.

Janie's cheeks heated. "Their spark isn't dying." If Keon didn't watch himself, *his* spark—as in his dastardly devilish wit—would get smothered to death. The new covers on the guest bed would do the job nicely. "You can't trick me into telling you what's inside." Neither could he outsmart her into exploring the contents further once she was alone. "I'll call Tania and deal with it. Honestly, Keon, just take your girl and go."

He gazed at her. "My girl?"

Janie blinked several times, the fluttering of her

eyelids embarrassingly reminiscent of a humming-bird flapping its wings. She willed the twitch to stop.

"T-T-T-T-Teacup," she stuttered. *Great.* Now she sounded like an insecure drummer introducing a beat into a song. "That's what you called her in the truck. Before you showed her the starfish. Your girl."

"Ah." His gaze lingered on Janie's face several heartbeats longer than necessary. "I remember it a little differently," he murmured, standing and placing down the dog. "Come on, girl."

The dog trotted behind him. He tugged the door partially closed.

Releasing a breath, Janie retrieved her phone and punched Tania's icon. She frowned as the ringing chimed in her ear.

What did he mean, he remembered their exchange *differently*?

In the living room, Keon arranged Trey's hardcover collection of classic detective fiction on a floating shelf, Teacup at his feet.

"Keon!" Janie's voice carried from the main

bedroom, where Tania had instructed her to unpack the box of mysteries. "Where's my phone?"

An amused smile curved his lips. Running his thumb along the spine of a slim volume, he shook his head. The woman would be the death of him, with her constant misplacing of electronics and her endearing cluelessness about how he felt. Since he'd left her to deal with the box, she'd lost her phone three times, requiring his help using the find-device app on her tablet or straightaway locating the cell himself.

Was she trying to torture him? Didn't she realize that whenever she sang out his name, cozy visions of the two of them preparing their own fantasy future home overflowed his mind? He wanted to make the most of their time together but couldn't shake the feeling he headed for another painful fall. Especially considering she hadn't gotten the hint in the truck that *she* was his girl.

Or, rather, he wished she was.

He slid the volume onto the shelf. Teacup scampering beside him, he entered the main bedroom. "Swipe your screen three times," he instructed Janie, stepping closer. "The find-phone icon is on the bottom row." He'd committed the spot to memory. If it were him, he would have moved the symbol to the first screen, but Janie had said doing so would make her app-reliant.

"I know where the icon is," she said, hands waving and bun bouncing, in a fluster. "That isn't the issue. My tablet battery died, and I forgot to pack the charger." Her index and middle fingers pinched together. "The cord was *right there* on the bench in my entryway."

"The farmhouse bench we found in that antique shop in Poulsbo?" He remembered their weekend away exploring the picturesque Washington town well. Janie had been over-the-top excited about finding the perfect piece for her foyer. Afterward, they'd enjoyed fresh, piping hot bread in a restaurant tucked on a side street before sharing a bottle of wine and a heaping platter of steamers. Later...well, he couldn't think about 'later' without obsessing about their steamy hours in bed.

She nodded. "My phone is older. I packed its charger, but it doesn't fit."

"I didn't bring a charger."

"Also, you plug in your phone every night," she said, as if the practice was incomprehensible. When they were a couple, he'd realized she waited until her batteries depleted to twenty percent before she charged her electronics. Whether the period between juicing lasted four hours or twenty-nine, for Janie, each break of dawn opened to another device adventure.

When would her battery die? Could she locate an outlet in time? Would not having her phone or tablet at her fingertips interrupt the task at hand or otherwise interject a hassle into her day?

Many, many, *many* times they'd discussed her—to his way of thinking—baffling habit. But honestly? Once he'd returned to Canada, he'd left his own phone unplugged now and then. Maybe as some sort of reminder or connection to this captivating woman.

Because, faced with the issue again in real time, Janie's ongoing refusal to shackle herself to the logic of a charging schedule had developed into another bewitching aspect of her charm.

He scanned the bedroom. "Your phone is on the dresser." He pointed.

She spotted the device. "Oh!" She slapped her forehead. "I'm losing it. Not the phone. My mind." She strode to the mirror-topped dresser and retrieved the gadget.

"Texting Tania?" he asked, noting the matching bedside lamps in the same muted shade of purple as the Russian sage plants sold at Hamaguchi's.

Bun wobbling, she shook her head. "No. Checking the couch delivery for tomorrow."

As she busied herself, Keon scanned the room again. Everything in Trey and Tania's inner sanctum as husband and wife appeared as if it had been plucked off an interior designer's website. Every stick of furniture, each decorative pillow, the two paintings on the far wall, and a pretty but impractical collection of vases on a tall chest of drawers, was brand new. From the purply-gray window coverings artfully draping the floor, to the upholstered headboard matching the fabric on the trunk at the foot of the bed, Janie had hung and positioned items in precise alignment. A silver picture frame with the words **OUR HONEYMOON** stamped on the bottom decorated one contemporary white nightstand, and a tissue-box cover in a similar style sat on the second.

Aside from the dog supplies piled in a corner, the room radiated magazine perfection. Almost as if the bride and groom were trying too hard. Keon couldn't imagine starting from scratch with brand-new stuff with his future wife. Wouldn't Janie want to include her farmhouse bench or the patchwork quilt that lay folded on her couch? Wouldn't his hiking gear require a corner of the closet?

He was getting ahead of himself again, daydreaming about What-Ifs.

Teacup woofed, and Keon glanced to his left as the animal trundled up the pet stairs positioned next to the upholstered trunk. Teacup centered herself on the piece of furniture and stretched her front paws onto Keon's legs. He scratched the pup behind her ears.

Finished checking the couch delivery, Janie stepped to the nightstand. Her phone dangled from her fingertips, hovering above the immaculate surface.

"I wouldn't do that," Keon advised before she set down the phone. "You might misplace it again."

She crossed her arms. "Like I'd forget my phone on the nightstand. It's an obvious spot."

And the dresser *hadn't* been? "Do what you want. I'm just going off how the day has played out."

"Where would you suggest I put it, oh, Favored One?"

Favored One? Was this some new hipster phrase he had yet to encounter? "In your jeans pocket. Last I checked, there were two of them back there."

She glanced around at her peach-shaped rear. "It'll stick out like a lump."

He laughed. "Who's looking?"

She peered at him sideways, as if to suggest *he* would.

"Ah, Janie." Absurdly pleased the notion had occurred to her, he smiled. "I know I was always particularly attracted to your butt, but I can restrain myself from ogling." Just barely.

She blinked. "Of course you can. We're apartment-prep coworkers."

"Yup." An invisible block of wood lodged in his throat. He gestured a hand between them. "Is this—are we—an issue for you, Janie?"

A tentative smile emerged. "I wouldn't say that. We're friends. I guess. Now that we've... broken the ice...there's no reason we can't stay out of the deep freeze once you're back in BC managing your business and enjoying your family, and I'm stuck here."

Stuck? "No, I suppose there isn't." Other than being around her, whether in real life or online, seemed destined to lead to increasingly deeper feelings on his end.

She slid her phone into her right back pocket. Humming, she zoned into hyper-focus mode, opening a moving box, lifting the box onto the bed, and pulling out her phone every few seconds, checking her notes and unloading items into dresser drawers.

Petting Teacup, Keon tracked her movements.

Janie looked up from a drawer. "Finished with the books?"

He nodded.

"Why not work in the guest room?"

"I'm allowed in there again?"

Pretty color splashed her cheeks. "Tania's box is dealt with."

"Her porn box?"

Janie's lips firmed. "*Keon.*"

He chuckled. "I'll take Teacup to the pet enclosure first."

"Yeah, that's probably a good idea." She stared at a drawer.

"Hey, girl," Keon said to the dog. "Want to go for a little walk?"

The Yorkie's ears perked. Janie's head swung back around, her not-missing-a-beat eyes focusing on the animal's antics as Teacup jumped into his arms.

"Careful," she admonished. "Minis have delicate bones."

"Can I help it if she loves me?"

Her lips twisted. "I guess not." Her gaze spun away again.

"I'll treat her like the princess she is," Keon promised, collecting Teacup's harness and leash and strapping her in safer than a skydiver with fifty jumps to her credit.

Recalling the strata rules, he carried the pup to the elevator. Outside, with Teacup's four paws and his two feet touching the ground, they strolled to the common grassy area. The cloudy skies cast a refreshing breeze over his T-shirt.

In the enclosure, Teacup emptied her bladder at the base of a massive oak tree and played with a cute pug. After fifteen minutes, he escorted the tuckered Yorkie back inside and settled her on her cushy living room bed.

Janie's head poked out of the primary bedroom. "You know what? I'll take her in here. I folded one of her blankets on top of the trunk. Tania said Teacup usually sleeps on the bottom of the bed and sneaks between their bodies at night. Once she and Trey move in, their goal is to encourage Teacup to move to the trunk and then to a doggy bed on the floor."

"All right." Keon wished the bride and groom the best of luck with that lofty aspiration.

Scooping up the sleepy dog, he transferred her to Janie. All four of Teacup's legs splayed like an untethered turkey sprawling in a roaster. Dog and woman vanished from sight.

Keon headed to the guest room on the other side of the kitchen. Not five minutes elapsed before he glimpsed Teacup wandering into the room. "T-Dog," he whispered. "Go back. Stay with Janie."

Teacup gazed at him with imploring brown eyes.

"Come on." He gathered the dog into his arms and returned her to the trunk as Janie emerged from the ensuite bathroom.

She frowned. "What's going on?"

"Teacup popped in to see me, that's all."

"Keon, don't tempt her."

He spread his hands palms-up, as if balancing plates. "I ain't done nothing."

She leveled him with a you're-testing-my-patience look. "Make sure it stays that way."

He saluted before returning to the guest room. Everything appeared in order. Entering the kitchen, he opened a box on the breakfast island containing cleaning paraphernalia intended for the main bathroom off the entry hall.

He took the box to the bathroom. Lowering to his knees, he arranged containers and soaps in the cabinet beneath the sink. Maybe three minutes had passed when, out of the corner of his eye, he spied a curious Yorkie dashing out of the primary bedroom toward him.

"Teacup," he whispered, leaning back on his heels and motioning the animal to stay back. "Go to Janie. Sleepy-sleep. Nappy-nap."

The dog stumbled over her paws in excitement, sliding on her haunches.

Keon laughed.

Janie showed up, concern written on her face and clear in her voice. "What am I going to do? She's infatuated with you."

Last summer, before returning home, Keon had written off his feelings—for the woman—in the same manner. What an idiot. "Too bad I only seem to have this problem with dogs."

She scoffed. "Right. How many women have you dated since we split? Four? Five?"

"We're going down this road? I was trying to forget you."

"That's neither here nor there. She and I"—Janie picked up Teacup—"need to bond." She kissed the dog's nose, and T-Dog's tiny tongue swiped at her cheek.

"That shouldn't be a problem," Keon said, stepping to within a few inches of the pair. "She just showed how much she likes you." He patted the dog's head.

"Not as much as she likes you," Janie said as Teacup wriggled and squirmed. She stroked the tiny dog, and Teacup settled.

"It's not a competition."

"It is when you factor in that she's staying with me during the honeymoon."

"Oh, yeah?" His chest warmed as he watched this knock-out woman and small animal interact. "When was this decided?"

"This morning, before you picked me up. I talked to Tania. She booked a trusted dog-sitter for Saturday and Sunday. The woman was supposed to take care of Teacup at the Hoyt house. Now, our girl is staying at the sitter's townhouse."

After the disaster with Mr. Sprinkles, that made sense. "Can't this person also take her during the honeymoon?"

Janie shook her head. "The sitter is booked solid, and our ladyship"—she smiled at Teacup, whose eyes grew sleepy—"isn't the sort to lump in with other dogs long term."

"Or cats," Keon remarked with a grin.

"*Especially* not cats." Janie kissed the dog's head. "You know what?" She looked at Keon. "You can help."

"Take care of her during the honeymoon?"

Chapter Eight

Bun wobbling, Janie hugged a drowsy Teacup to her chest. Had any wax remaining in her ears, which she'd cleaned last week, thank you very much, magically transformed into voice-muffling capsules? Had her ex-boyfriend suggested he continue throwing her world into turmoil by staying in Rosevale to... to...take care of Tania and Trey's *dog*?

Yes, Janie had dreamed about the stud-dude extending his time in town. Or, in her wildest imaginings, having never left. What woman wouldn't? The man standing in front of her with an oh-shoot-I've-done-it-now expression on his handsome face was a tall, sexy, charismatic drink of water.

But no good would come of Keon extending his

visit. Venturing down that road would only end in more pain and heartache. One way or another, Janie needed him gone. Her heart hammered. *After* the wedding.

Whatever conclusions they drew about their relationship and, she realized with dreadful certainty, they needed to dig deeper than she'd anticipated, they must draw a conclusion. How else could either of them move forward?

"Excuse me?" she asked in a wary tone. "Keon, no. I meant, help me organize the main bedroom. Why would you, um, say what you did?"

"Forget it." His face reddened. "It was a slip of the tongue."

He had that right. "I need to move beyond the concept of you and me," Janie explained. "Please say you understand that."

His jaw moved jerkily up and down, as if wire held his joints together. "I do now."

But his gaze radiated otherwise. Every time he looked at her longer than a quarter of a second, the longing in his eyes made her tummy flip.

"I care for you," Janie stressed. "I always will. But we were meant for a good time, not a long time. Remember?" Foolish thinking, she realized now.

"Hey." He smiled. "I'm game for a good time."

Her chin pulled back at his surprise answer. Careful not to startle the dog, she whispered, "You're suggesting we *sleep together* for old time's sake?"

"No?" he responded like an ever-hopeful, red-blooded twenty-nine-year-old man. "Unless, well, you're suggesting it."

"I'm not." Although, a traitorous part of her would love nothing more. She needed to beat that wench down. Keep her locked in the captain's cabin on the pirate ship—with the captain on the other side of the door. Luckily, in this analogy, the key remained hidden in a secret spot the captain would never discover. Besides, Janie's fantasy captain was a gentleman. Who bore a passing resemblance to the man standing two feet away.

"Janie," he said softly. "I get it. I do." He nodded at Teacup. "Look."

Janie dropped her gaze to the dog nestled dead asleep against her thundering heart.

"See?" He stepped closer. "She likes you."

"I need to put her down somewhere," she whispered, looking at Keon but avoiding eye contact. Considering her reaction to the man, staring into his deep brown irises might hypnotize her into recon-sidering the location of the imaginary cabin key. "Then we can keep on-schedule. With the move-in." Best to make her meaning perfectly clear.

He pointed to the nearby pet bed. "Should we leave her here, in the living room?"

Janie shook her head. "Let's try the trunk." Where the bride and groom eventually wanted Teacup to sleep most nights.

"*Let's?*" he echoed. "As in, you want *me* to go into Trey and Tania's bedroom with you...two?" His finger twirled, indicating the dog.

Janie frowned. Hadn't she just said that? "Teacup has latched onto you like a bloodhound on a scent. If you're not close, she might wake up." The success of this week depended on them completing specific tasks per day. If one to-do list veered off-track, a disastrous domino effect might occur.

"All right." His hand settled on the small of her back.

This is for Tania, this is for Tania, she reminded herself, inching ahead of him as they entered the bedroom. She placed the snoozing dog on the blan-ket-topped trunk.

"I still don't understand why newlyweds would

want a dog anywhere near the mattress," he groused.

"When Trey is out of town, Teacup sleeps *on* the bed. With Tania."

"That's too confusing. How do they expect her to change to the trunk?"

"Not our issue." Janie resumed unpacking the bride's belongings. "You do Trey's," she directed.

Nodding, he worked at the tall dresser while she emptied items into the wide, low one. Minutes later, she gave his progress a cursory glance. Teacup's head lifted. The animal's groggy gaze tracked his movements.

It's not my fault, Keon mouthed to Janie.

"Ignore her," Janie whispered. "She'll sack out." She would cross her eyes and her fingers to increase the chances, if she thought it would help.

Two minutes later, a snuffling noise prompted her to check on Teacup again. The dog journeyed down the pet stairs!

Keon collected the pooch, returned her to the trunk, folded the portable steps, and placed them aside. "Stay," he commanded the animal. "Nappy-nap."

At the gentle sound of his voice, something gooey mushed inside Janie. The dog yawned, snout flopping onto her paws, and Janie and Keon got back to work.

Another minute later, Teacup's head sprang up when the Favored One, carrying handfuls of Trey's belongings, passed Tania's dresser on his way into the walk-in closet. Heart hammering, Janie intercepted the dog preparing to jump *off* the trunk. She held the exasperating creature in front of her nose.

"Imp, you'll be the death of me," she muttered.

Teacup yawned, her spindly hind legs dangling.

Keon reemerged. "What have we here?"

"A challenge in perseverance, Yorkie-style. Look, I'm nearly done arranging Tania's dresser. I'll cuddle this one on the bed." She nodded at Teacup. "You finish Trey's."

Keon shrugged. "All right."

No, not *all right*. They risked falling behind, but Teacup had proven herself a tenacious adversary. Janie either needed to slip the pooch a sedative—which, no, she would *never*—or otherwise facilitate the bonding process.

She deposited the dog on the foot of the bed. Then, after lying down with her head on Tania's designated pillow, bun squashed between her temple and the mega-thread-count pillowcase, she patted the mattress in invitation for the animal to join her.

Barking, Teacup bounded up and curled beneath her arm. Janie grinned. *Hah, fooled you, girl. Yorkie-trainers, take note.*

"Shh," she whispered, kissing the dog's ears. Soon, a contented snuffle-snoring sound revealed that the devil-princess had fallen asleep. "Thank God," Janie murmured before allowing her own eyes to close.

The sounds of Keon moving around the large bedroom echoed in the quiet space, and before too long a sense of deep contentment settled over her. It wouldn't hurt if she imagined this was *their* room, and this dog, their dog, and this coming wedding—

She mentally stomped the thought into dust.

Keon's activity reached her ears again. A sigh drifted from her mouth. A comfortable darkness enshrouded her, and the temptation to nod off grew. What would it hurt if she gave in to the exhaustion of the week for a spell?

Her arm relaxed over Teacup's warm body as her head sank into the downy softness of the pillow, her mind initially wandering and then giving way to a sensation of floating in a pleasurable wake of images of rolling hills, a sparkling lake, and a flower shop called Janie's Blossoms. The hand-carved wooden sign hanging above the open archway that led from the indoor portion of Hamaguchi's Fruit and Garden Centre—spelled the Canadian way, ending in RE—featured daisies and butterflies and tiny, chirping birds. The sort one might find in an animated fairy tale.

A fuzzy feeling invaded her consciousness, and the skin of her forehead puckered. Why were the birds chirping? Was the sign electrical? Who had ordered a garish neon sign with irritating twittering birds?

The thoughts disturbed the tranquility of her meditative state, so it didn't bother her one iota when a nearby shiny bubble burst into a panorama of her first customer paying for her first prepared order of bright yellow daffodils and pale pink tulips.

It didn't feel strange or out of place when Keon appeared behind the cash register, embracing her as they kissed.

A sudden, urgent satisfaction buoyed by a happiness and joy she had never experienced seemed natural and necessary and everything she had ever yearned for. If not for those darn chirping—

"Janie?" Keon's voice battled through the layers

of fluffy cotton balls plugging her brain. "Your phone."

"It's chirping?" she asked, heavy eyelids peeling open.

He stood beside the night table, Teacup in his arms. "Your brother's number flashed on the screen."

She sat up, bun drooping. "I'll call him later." Right now, she had more urgent business to attend to. She wagged a finger at the dog. "You were supposed to stay on the bed. With me."

Keon smiled. "You were napping. She woke and walked in a circle, as if she needed to pee. I took her to the sunroom patch. She squatted."

Janie put a hand to her upper chest. "*I* should have taken her."

"It was no big deal."

"It is to me." She blew out a breath. "This isn't working."

"Janie, lie back down," Keon whispered, petting the dog. "She needs incentive."

"She needs *you*." That was becoming plain as day.

He hesitated. "How about if we both...rest...on the bed with her?"

The dog's ears twitched.

Janie worried her lower lip between her teeth.

Cradling the dog one-handed, Keon walked to the trunk, retrieved the small blanket, and transferred the cover to the bottom of the bedspread. "Is this how Tania does it?"

"For the nights Trey is in town, yes."

"Okay," he responded in a reasonable tone. "If we can get Teacup feeling comfortable with you and me as a pair, then in a day or two she'll progress to bonding with you."

Janie narrowed her gaze. She didn't know about this.

Keon shot her a glance. "If you have another idea, I'm all ears. I'm trying to find a solution that will ultimately help *you*, Janie, when you're caring for her on your own. I suppose you could tough it out, turn your head when she paws and whines—and don't forget the stress-chewing on your coffee table legs, the passive-aggressive urinating anywhere but on the grass patch, and maybe a dung heap deposited here and there—until she collapses into an unhappy pile of scruff in your apartment. Or, worse, in Roslyn's store."

Janie's nose wrinkled. He painted a putridly precise picture.

"It's up to you," he ended with a shrug.

Janie scoured her Alternate Ideas bank, but it was empty. Giving a curt nod, she announced, "Trey sleeps on the right, farthest from the bathroom." She lay down again, on her back this time, staring at the ceiling, hands folded on her stomach, as stiff as a corpse in a viewing casket.

Keon settled the dog on the blanket at the foot of the mattress. Teacup snuffled her nose into the creases before curling into a snoring ball.

Janie glanced at Trey's half of the bed as Keon sat on the bedspread and positioned himself on his side with his back to her.

She gulped. "Tania once mentioned that they sleep...facing each other."

"A detail."

"It might be important." If they were doing this, they were doing it right.

Keon rolled over, his gaze meeting hers. He inserted one of his hands beneath his head on the pillow. The other rested on the bedspread. "You're on your back."

Janie looked at the ceiling. "I know," she replied in a hushed voice.

"Shouldn't you face me?" he whispered. His finger poked her shoulder. "Janie?"

"I will, I will. In a second." Summoning courage,

she squeezed shut her eyes. They hadn't lain this close to each other in over a year. And...she missed it. She missed being with him. Not only having sex, although that part of their relationship had been outstanding. But sharing the same bed countless times throughout those early-summer nights. Waking in his arms in the gentle light of morning. Laughing and teasing and feeling a part of something. A part of *someone*.

That he had felt like a part of *her*.

She inhaled a shallow breath. Oh, God, why had she allowed herself to fall in love with him back then?

She struggled not to cry out with the intensity of the raw emotions burning her throat. Now, was she *still* in love with Keon? Regardless of every rational reason not to be?

Had she fooled herself all these months? Would a part of her heart always belong to him? Even if one day she maneuvered her way into falling in love with somebody else?

Keon was her first real love.

Not a crush. Not infatuation.

She *loved* him.

The ache in her chest released.

Maybe, for her, that was how things were.

Maybe some lucky people carried a special love throughout their lives, even as they joined paths with a totally different person.

And that was okay.

Because Janie now knew that she was one of those incredibly lucky souls.

She opened her eyes.

Chapter Nine

Studying Janie's profile on the pillow, Keon willed her to stop fighting the inevitable, turn her head, allow her gaze to travel the three hand spans of space and look at him.

Really look.

At *him*.

It wasn't enough that she'd opened her eyes. It was confusing as hell that she'd instructed him to roll over and then had purposely obstructed his view into the mirrors of her soul to where she'd compressed her pretty peepers as if she were a warrior steeling for battle.

What in the world was running through her mind?

He cast a glance at the foot of the bed. "Janie," he

whispered. "Teacup is asleep." His suggestion that they both lay down had worked.

Her breasts rose and fell in her bright blue T-shirt as she drew in another long breath. "Keon," she whispered before finally, *finally* angling her head his way.

Air sluiced into his lungs. He wasn't aware of having inhaled. But his chest suddenly felt inflated to bursting. Warmth and tenderness radiated from her thick-lashed eyes. Had he never noticed this expressive emotion reflecting from her features before?

It was more intense than fondness.

Greater than affection.

Stretching beyond physical attraction.

Yes, he *had* sensed this feeling before, he realized, pleasure coursing through his veins. Other times, the look had quickly come and gone, occurring occasionally when they were dating. Gracing her smiles and glances during their last morning in her apartment. Then later, the same emotion, tinged with sadness, shone from her face as they said goodbye at Sea-Tac Airport.

"Look at you," he whispered, fingers itching to touch her, arms pining to hold her. He remained motionless.

"Look at me?" she whispered, sounding confused.

"Janie, you're—" He needed to express some of what he was feeling. Not enough to scare her off. "You're beautiful," he whispered. Her bun had loosened, and several sandy-blond strands curled against her neck.

Her gaze shuttered. "Keon."

"No. Please. Don't close yourself off." Love swelled beneath his breastbone. That he loved Janie McAllister wasn't in question any longer. His love for her infused his cells, and he was tired of pretending he possessed the strength to punch it down.

Moments ago, she'd said they needed to face each other. It was clear she'd intended the phrase literally.

But they needed to reach that point in their relationship as well.

Before he left Rosevale, he and Janie needed to come to terms with what they felt for each other. Nothing less would satisfy him.

"I won't touch you," he whispered. Although he wanted to. How he wanted to. "I only want to say how much I've missed you all this time. Since I moved home."

Her lashes swept downward. "Same," she said, as if the admission physically hurt.

"You don't look very comfortable," he teased. She'd rotated her neck but continued to lie on her back, her bun squashed between her cheek and the pillow. "Are you sure this is what you meant when you said Tania and Trey sleep facing each other?"

"Tania sleeps in a mirror image of Trey," she replied softly. "They both sleep on their sides, toward each other. Tania told me once when we were discussing...such matters."

Like Janie's preferred side for sleeping next to him? "Oh, I get it. You're improvising. After making *me* turn over completely, you've decided you're only halfway in."

"I'm all in."

"If that were true, you'd lay on your side, like me." Mimicking the positions of the future married couple.

"Keon." Janie rolled her eyes. "Very well," she said in a prim voice, moving onto her arm and hip, facing him on the expensive-looking bedspread. His throat tightened as her gaze swept over his face. "This is weird," she whispered. "Going horizontal on the bride and groom's new bed feels sacrilegious."

He chuckled. "Tania wants us to make sure the mattress is comfortable, right?"

"Actually, she asked me to test it out. Me," she emphasized, middle finger tapping her chest.

"When did she add this vital task to your colossal list of instructions?"

"Weeks ago."

"There you go. Before I became your assistant. Now that I am, she must realize you might delegate some chores."

"You have me there," Janie replied in an amused tone.

"As I see it, you needed to test the new mattress to determine if it meets the bride and groom's specified standards. And I'm helping, magnanimous fellow that I am." Grinning, he patted the bedspread between their bodies. "In case we need to send this one back and request a replacement."

Appearing more at ease now, Janie giggled. "You can rationalize anything."

Yet, somehow, he hadn't rationalized away his attachment to this bewitching thief of his heart.

"Your bun is falling apart," he said, changing subjects to prevent himself from veering into too-deep-too-soon territory.

"It's a fashion choice. I call it The Teacup."

He tamped down the laughter rumbling in his chest.

"It *is* uncomfortable." She reached up and loosened the pins and an elastic. Rolling toward the nightstand on her side of the bed, she set the items in a decorative dish before facing him again. Her messy hair fell sexily around her face and over her shoulders.

He risked a slight conversation swerve. "We need to talk."

She swallowed. "We do."

Relief whooshed through him. "The last thing I want is to overwhelm you, but I can't go home next week without telling you—" *How much I love you.*

But today was not the day to delve into those fiery depths.

"Go ahead, Keon," she whispered, her bottom lip quivering. "We can discuss this."

Discuss it, yes. Profess his undying love? Not yet. *It's too soon.* "If not for me returning to Canada, would we have...do you think..."

She nodded. "We would have kept dating."

His voice grew gruff. "I developed feelings for you last summer."

A fine sheen of tears dampened her eyes. "Same."

His pulse pounded. He inched his hand toward hers on the bedspread but didn't make contact. Her fingers twitched. He said, "From your perspective, once I returned home, it might have felt like I didn't care."

"Because your dance card filled within weeks?" She gave a half-smile.

He hadn't the faintest idea what a dance card was, but guessed it represented his social life. "I dated a lot. I'm not denying that. I didn't mean to hurt you by looking around. I meant it when I said I was trying to forget you." He waited a beat. "Didn't you date anyone?"

Her gaze lowered. "A couple of guys. After I realized you'd moved on."

"I wouldn't say 'moved on,' exactly." Not emotionally, that was for sure.

She looked up. "All right, if we're splitting hairs, it seemed like you recovered a lot faster from our breakup than I did. But it wasn't the same. Neither of those guys were you."

Another wave of relief washed through him. They shared the same sentiment. "Did you—?" He shook his head. "Sorry. It's not my business." He wasn't jealous. He had no right.

"Sleep with anyone? I don't mind telling you. I

didn't." Her shoulders lifted and fell against the bedspread. "Those guys were nice, good-looking, in shape, employed." One corner of her mouth curved upward. "Perfect for me, aside from not being you. And I have a fourth-date rule." She tugged her bottom lip between her teeth, her gaze searching his face. "Neither guy lasted four dates."

Four dates? "Is that the same as a three-date rule?" In one word, sex.

She nodded, head moving on her pillow. "I reserve the three-date guideline for the super-hot."

Keon squinted. "I don't remember us waiting for a fourth date." Or a third date. Or a second. Not even a first. They'd decided to keep seeing each other following their hookup, which, in retrospect, counted as a first date.

Liquid softness entered her eyes. Her fingers moved a centimeter closer to his on the bedspread. "There you have it," she said huskily. "Super-duper-hot. Plus, we already knew each other. We had the same friends."

A smile spread across his lips. "I'm so glad I sat on your blanket that night." At the outdoor concert with their crowd. He hadn't been able to resist the merriment in her expression, the scent of strawberries glossing her lips, the bees-and-daisies clips in her hair. That night, everything he'd considered allowing himself to feel for this woman had coalesced into zings of physical and emotional attraction.

"I'm glad you did too," she whispered. "Remember when Heath tripped over us? It was cloudy. No stars or moonlight. It was very dark."

Keon chuckled. "He was a little drunk." The goof, returning from the portable toilets set up for the concertgoers, stumbled on a depression in the grass. Keon, focused on Janie, hadn't spotted the potential danger. The resulting impact toppled both him and Janie over, and they'd capsized onto her woven Mexican blanket, limbs tangling. Heat had burst in him at every point of contact.

Janie's friends jumped to their rescue. After checking that no one was hurt, her friends returned to their spots. Keon, desperate for another touch of her, sat closer to her on the blanket. Over the next hour, their hands, arms, and legs grazed several times.

Eventually, his fingers lingered on hers. She grasped his hand loosely. He caressed her knuckles, and she adjusted her position. He entwined their hands on her thigh, and they hadn't let go again until the concert ended and they packed up their stuff.

He drove her home, and the rest was history. They woke in bed together and were a couple from that point forward.

Until they weren't.

"Janie, I should tell you." He paused. "I slept with someone before Christmas, and I slept with Danika." His last girlfriend.

Her gaze didn't waver. "It's okay. You never said you were a monk. We each said we'd move on. I just didn't."

"Still. I feel bad. My heart wasn't in it. I thought, this is my last swing at bat."

Her glance shot to his jeans zipper. "Is that a metaphor?"

He laughed. "Danika is a nice person. She deserves happiness. It wasn't right taking things to the next level with her when, in the end, I realized I was hoping she'd help me get over you."

"I'll bet she reacted well to *that* news."

"It was a jerk move."

"Agreed." But Janie smiled.

"Luckily, she forgave me." Keon hesitated. His neck stiffened even while his head remained on the down-filled pillow. "Janie," he ventured. "I tried to forget us, and I hurt at least one person. But I was lost. There's no one at home like you."

"There's no one here like you," she whispered, breath feathering from her pink lips.

"That leaves us in a quandary."

Her gaze locked with his, the spellbinding skies of her eyes stealing his heart.

"What should we do about it?" she asked, voice barely above a whisper.

"Deal with our feelings as best as we can." Until he was prepared to confess that she was it for him.

"Instead of burying them? Because that doesn't seem to be working out."

He nodded. "I want to touch you," he said hoarsely.

Her smile brightened her beautiful face. "I want to touch you too."

He rested a hand on her shoulder, his thumb grazing the sleeve of her T-shirt and his fingers brushing the silky flesh of her arm. "Is this okay?"

"Yes." She scooted closer.

They caressed each other's backs and shoulders. His body hardened.

"How about this?" he asked, lifting a hand to stroke Janie's hair and then her cheek.

"*Yes.*" The warmth of her face curved against his palm. Her lips parted.

His ribs constricted. He brought his mouth to hers and savored a year-in-the-waiting sip of her sweetness.

Teacup roused from slumber. The dog's half-woof-half-yawn reverberated in the quiet bedroom.

Janie and Keon chuckled. As they gazed at each other, the dog walked up the bed to stand behind Janie. The animal examined her quizzically.

"She's giving me the hairy eyeball, isn't she?" she asked, and Keon nodded.

Her shoulders shook as she restrained a chuckle.

After a few seconds, Teacup lifted her forepaws and hiked over Janie's hips and then Keon's. The tiny dog paced behind his back before lying down and plastering her warm belly against his spine. The sharp claws of one paw poked his backbone.

Janie grinned. "She's telling us to exercise caution. We should only take things so far."

"I can't disagree." For one thing, this was the bride and groom's new bed. Tania and Trey should be the ones to break it in. "I don't want to violate newlywed-apartment protocol," he whispered, cupping Janie's chin, "but I really, really want to kiss you again."

"I really, really want to kiss you."

"A gentle kiss." He swallowed the lump in his throat, which was paltry compared to the bump in his jeans. He couldn't handle a feverish kiss right now. But he craved a close connection with his love.

"No tongue," Janie whispered, teasingly referring to his 'slip of the tongue' comment earlier. "If you can restrain herself."

"You doubt my ability?"

Her eyebrows arched.

"Challenge accepted." Their lips met, moving tenderly. Heat flooded—and floored—Keon. Her sunshiny scent filled his head as her soft breasts crushed against his chest. He fit her pelvis snug against him, his hands on her rear. She shifted her hips, her top leg hooking over his and the bowl of her body cradling him.

Her hips slowly gyrated, and she moaned.

"Janie," he whispered, hands in her hair. He loved her. He yearned to shout the truth from a mountaintop. She was the only woman for him.

His person.

His partner.

He needed her.

He craved her.

He adored her.

But even as their bodies clamored, their relationship remained in limbo. Would it be enough? Was what they had in this moment the most he could wish for?

Was it fair to tell her...now, tomorrow, the day he left...how he felt? That he'd fallen in love with her during his year in Washington? That he still loved her?

He hadn't 'developed feelings,' damn it. *He loved her.*

Groaning, he deepened the kiss.

She panted. "Is your tongue slipping again?" she whispered.

"What?"

"Into my mouth this time," she teased.

He smiled. "Do you want it to slip?" he asked, kissing the tip of her nose.

She gazed into his eyes, vulnerability reflecting in her open expression. "Until Monday," she whispered. "When you fly home."

Chapter Ten

THE NEXT AFTERNOON, Janie soaked in the sight of Keon's muscular calves and mighty fine backside in pocketed navy shorts as he accompanied the sofa delivery team to the apartment entryway. Her heart squeezed as he chatted and laughed with the burly men in his friendly, outgoing manner. He really was an exceptional guy, and happiness bubbled within her that they'd found their way back to each other, however temporary the situation.

She refused to dwell on the coming pain and heartache when she said goodbye to him again. She just wanted to enjoy this time.

Their time. Live for the moment, not worry about tomorrow, all that jazz.

It was liberating.

At the sound of the entryway door clicking shut, she glanced around the living room, hand to her heart. Not only was her newfound romantic philosophy vibing, but the condo-prep gods must be smiling on her, because the living room furniture looked perfect. Exactly as ordered. Not one thing wrong.

Over the last hour, under her direction and as per Tania's wishes, Keon helped the delivery guys arrange the coffee and side tables in a visually pleasing arrangement along with the love seat and sofa. The upmarket dining table and chairs sat tucked beneath a corner window. Some final touches to the primary bathroom, the electronics for the living room and bedrooms, the plants Keon would drive from Trey's old place, and picking up the rattan furniture for the sunroom remained.

A sudden smattering of nerves chased around in her tummy, and she chewed a thumbnail. Tomorrow was Thursday, and Friday included the bridesmaid spa date, the wedding rehearsal, and the dinner. She hadn't gotten ahead of herself and jinxed the next forty-eight hours, had she?

"Don't worry unless you want to break out in warts," she whispered beneath her breath. If that wasn't a saying, it should be.

Keon returned from the foyer, smile wide. "We're making great headway." He slipped a hand around her waist.

She released a soft exhale. "We are." Swiveling in his embrace, she welcomed the kisses he dropped to her mouth. Yesterday, when he drove her home, she hadn't invited him into her apartment. He'd needed to take Teacup back to Heath's and catch up on management tasks for the garden center.

She sighed as his lips slid over hers. As much as she longed to make love with this man for the first time in a year, dare she jeopardize what they shared for an ultra-satisfying roll in the hay?

Giddy as she felt in his arms, if they decided on vying for some action, what about the timing? Tonight, at her apartment? Tomorrow, after he checked into the wedding hotel?

Or was it wiser not to make love at all during this precious handful of days? To wait and see how their relationship progressed?

That was, *if* their romance progressed. He hadn't said another word about extending his visit. After nixing the idea, she didn't know if she had the guts to reinstate the subject.

Her pulse sped up. Wait, she was living *for the moment*, remember?

"You look like you're popping out of your skin," he murmured, forehead touching hers as he kissed the tip of her nose, a classic Rivers move that never failed to weaken her knees.

She ran her hands up and down his muscular forearms. "I'm excited."

His dark eyebrows quirked. "About?"

You. This. Us.

"That today has gone so well." She brushed back her loose hair and smoothed the soft hem of her sweatpants-style shorts. "The deliveries, the set-up. That the devil-princess has cut us some slack." Teacup was on her best behavior. The dog napped on her pet bed in the sunroom. Janie had cracked open the French doors after Keon and the guys finished arranging the furniture, but the Yorkie continued to snooze away the afternoon bathed in an amber splash of sunshine.

"She's exhausted. Heath took her to a dog park before work. He introduced her to at least a dozen canines."

"I'm taking the imp's cooperation more as a sign that she and I have finally bonded." Which boded well for Janie, considering she was pet sitting the dog during the honeymoon.

"Of course you have. Who wouldn't want to bond with you, Janie? You're wonderful."

Tingles raced across her chest. Returning to the safety of furniture talk, she twirled away while clasping Keon's hand, as if they were a matched-for-years figure-skating pair. "Be that as it may," she gushed, "it's almost unbelievable that the couch is the correct shade of tan." She skimmed her free palm along the back of the three-seater sofa. Tania and Trey had chosen an attractive caramel-colored leather, but Tania had worried the order might accidentally revert to their original cigar shade. "The throw pillows look fabulous."

"And the mattress in their bedroom has the perfect amount of bounce," Keon contributed, humor brimming his voice.

Janie laughed. Yesterday, they'd made out for an hour on that mattress, a fancy hybrid memory foam thing. "Tania can never know what happened in their private sanctuary."

The man she adored tugged her into his arms. He twirled her to the front of the two-seater sofa, and they sank onto the expansive cushions.

"What would she do?" he asked, nibbling her neck.

"Freak out?" Janie whispered as a shivery sensation swept her limbs.

He pulled her onto his lap. His erection bulged in his shorts, and the zipper grazed the exposed flesh of her thighs.

"I feel guilty," she admitted, kissing him before ducking her head.

"For what?" he asked, voice raspy.

She wriggled against his arousal. "Turning you on but keeping you at bay."

His chuckle rumbled low and deep in his throat. "I don't mind if we take things slow. Other parts—" his glance arrowed toward his lap "—have their own ideas."

"*Their*? There's two?"

He laughed. "Two of one thing, one of another. I can't control my physical reaction to you, Janie."

Again, she sighed as his mouth took hers in another long, drugging kiss.

Coming up for air, she planted a palm against his T-shirt. His heart pounded beneath her touch. She ventured, "You're honestly okay not knowing when we might take this to a bed?"

"More than okay. I won't lie. I want you. A hell of a lot." His fingers danced over her hip and inched beneath the hem of her shorts, along her sensitized skin. Desire bloomed, liquid in her veins. His fingers traipsed out again. "I'd hoped to reconnect with you," he said, gazing into her eyes. "I wished with all my heart to feel close to you again. But I didn't expect my feelings to come on this strongly, and I don't want to pressure you."

"Same. I don't want to move too fast and ruin what we have. I want to enjoy us."

"I want to enjoy *you*," he whispered, hand firm on the middle of her back as his mouth lowered to within a hairsbreadth of hers. "I understand that might not mean home base."

"*Keon*," she murmured, hungering for his kiss.

His tongue swept into her mouth. One of his hands molded her breasts through her button-front crop top. His fingers skated beneath the ribbed fabric, slipped inside her bra, and caressed her nipple. "Janie." His erection jutted, and her passion for him grew.

"Keon, that feels so good. Wait—" If she didn't take control, they might blast newlywed-apartment protocol to smithereens.

Changing positions, she straddled his lap. Knees digging into the cushions and fingertips lovingly brushing his whisker stubble, she moved her hips and kissed him.

"What's this now?" His voice sounded guttural.

"I thought you'd like a lap dance."

"I'd love a lap dance. But if this is your idea of moving slow…"

She ground against his zipper. "I want you to feel good."

"I feel amazing, honey. But I need to hang the TVs and install the sound system." His lips grazed her hair, and he swore. "I can't believe I said that."

"Mr. Responsibility." She loved that about him.

"You have stuff to do in the ensuite, right?"

Straightening on his lap, Janie giggled. "What?"

"The bathroom. In the primary bedroom. You know, they walk *into* the bathroom *from* the bedroom. Hence, the *ensuite*."

"Ensuite," she echoed, lips curving. "I love your Canadianisms." She undulated her hips against his Canadianism.

"Ensuite is a Canadianism?" he choked out. "Who knew?"

"We are more likely to say, 'attached bath.'"

"But the bathroom is an offshoot."

"Let's take 'suite' in another direction," she whispered. "Your kisses are sweet. S-W-E-E-T sweet," she spelled, brushing a caress against his mouth. "Your hands are sweet."

"S-W-E-E-T sweet?"

Nodding, she placed his hands on her hips.

"Your kisses are *hot*," he said as her phone on the breakfast island played the opening strains of the wedding march. "That's a mother-in-law-from-hell notification," he added in mock terror.

She laughed. "It's Tania's latest text tone for the bridesmaids. Apparently, some of us weren't responding quickly enough."

In another second, his phone on the side table flashed a video-call notification from the groom.

"Talk about a buzzkill," Janie murmured, sliding off his lap and walking to the island to check her phone.

Visualizing a weed-whacker trimming his 'garden,' Keon cupped a hand over his shorts and adjusted his stuff. As the situation in his shorts diminished, he plucked his phone off the side table, but didn't tap the icon to bring in Trey.

Janie strode back from the breakfast island, gaze on her device. "Tania says they want to video-chat."

"With me?" Keon asked as his phone chimed.

Good thing he'd purchased a robust data package to use in the US.

"Both of us. If we're together." She smiled. "Which we are."

He liked the way she said that. *Both of us. Together.* He nodded.

Typing a message, she glanced at his lap. "I said you're in the bathroom. That Trey should wait and not cancel the call." She placed her phone in a wavy glass bowl on the coffee table.

"Good idea," he replied, scanning her curves—but not long enough to repack wood. "Straighten your top." One shoulder of the garment drooped, flashing a bra strap. The hem swished at the indentation of her trim waist. "And fetch Teacup. Please," he added, sounding like he was choking on lust. Which, suddenly, he was. Again.

Eyes sparkling, she tidied her clothes. "Ready?"

"As long as we don't aim the camera at my lap," he said as she retrieved the dog. Moments ago, when she'd straddled him, her hair cascading over her shoulders and a flowery perfume scenting the skin behind her ears, her pale gray shorts had felt as soft as his favorite sweatpants beneath his fingers but possessed the benefit of revealing toned female legs.

Flat sandals completed her outfit, showcasing her painted toenails.

How could this woman look casual, cute, and knock-him-dead gorgeous at the same time?

She tumbled Teacup onto his lap. He winced as the dog pressed a paw into just the right—or was that *not* right?—spot.

"Thanks. I guess. Ouch."

Her cheeks pink, Janie sat. "Sorry."

"No problem." Not anymore. As the dog curled into a ball, he thumbed his phone. "Hi," he greeted when the bride and groom's smiling faces appeared. The small corner image bisected Janie's features. Keon extended the camera's reach, and a view of her head emerged.

She waved at Trey and Tania, who relaxed on the couch in their old place.

Tania beamed. "Hi, you two."

Trey looped an arm around his bride. "I grabbed the rest of the day off, so we thought we'd check in. How are things going? With the dog and setting up our new home?"

Janie clasped Keon's hand, and the heat of her touch sparked embers on his skin. Maintaining skin-to-skin contact, she rotated the phone to capture Teacup in the frame.

Tania squealed. "Tea-baby!"

"As you can see, your dog is happy," Janie said with a smile.

T-Dog bounced around on Keon's lap, barking. "For the sake of my future children, Teacup is going on the floor," he noted dryly, ceding control of his phone to Janie and lowering the dog. The Yorkie pounced onto a toy and romped.

Janie swiveled the camera back around to reflect their faces in the corner again.

"You two are sweet." Tania slapped Trey's thigh. "I *knew* it would happen if we gave it half a chance."

Trey's eyebrows twitched, and Keon peered at his longtime friends. Was Tania referring to Janie and Teacup bonding? Or to Janie and...him?

His apartment-prep partner took the comment in stride. "Everything is perfect," she enthused, standing to sweep the camera over the new furniture. The dog raced into the sunroom, toy cheeping.

"It looks amazing." Tania's excitement emanated from the phone. "Thanks, guys."

"One more day, and we're done." Janie returned to the loveseat, the phone propped against the bowl.

Tania wriggled. "I can't believe how close we are to moving in. It's exciting."

Trey nodded. "Have you met any neighbors?"

A placid expression fell over Janie's features. "Natalie and Mariah," she informed the couple. "This guy named Hugh, and Madge and her husband. Madge is fond of strata rules."

"There's always one," Trey remarked at the same time Tania said, "Wow, you had quite the party."

"I'll tell you about it sometime," Janie promised, placing a hand on Keon's thigh. His muscles warmed to her touch even as guilt for their subterfuge wormed beneath his skin.

Trey grinned. "It's great to see you two getting along, by the way."

Tania's eyes widened. She elbowed Trey.

"Why wouldn't we get along?" Janie asked.

Tania twirled an earring. "No reason. Only because...you know..."

Trey planted his hands on his knees, leaning forward. "Let's not pussyfoot around. Because you two broke up."

Tania's eyes assumed a glassy sheen. "Now you have to spend all this time together. Because of *our* apartment. And *our* dog." She sounded like a social media influencer promoting her favorite sitcom.

"We're concerned it might be an issue," Trey said.

Keon poked a thumb into his chest. "It's not an issue for me."

"Me neither," Janie said. "It's not an issue for me." She shook her head.

Keon glanced at her. She didn't sound or look convinced.

Trey leaned back. "Glad to hear it. Send pictures of Teacup every day while we're gone, okay?"

Janie lifted a finger. "Definitely. Is that all?" Her smile appeared frozen in place.

Trey chuckled. "What did I tell you, Keon?"

Damned if he knew.

"He's talking about ages ago," Tania added. "Come on. You guys know."

"Know what?" Keon asked, eyebrows bunching. His thoughts remained stuck on Janie's curious response to Trey, as well as her shocked expression.

Tania gave a now-I-have-to-spell-it-out look. "Everyone in the friend group adores you two as a couple. Keon and Janie. Janie and Keon. We miss Jay-On." She pouted. "But this isn't about us." She lovingly smacked Trey's shoulder. "It's about you two."

Janie inhaled. "Tania. Are you meddling?"

"Me? Hah! No, no. Nope. I need you to do this thing for us."

Trey said, "*The Last Chance for Bromance* golf shirts for Friday need picking up."

"I meant to get them this afternoon," Tania said. "But now Trey and I..." She mimed turning an invisible key into a lock against her lips.

Trey's eyebrows waggled. "We want to enjoy being engaged tonight, if you know what I mean. Starting," he glanced at his watch, "when this call ends. And then, however many times we can fit in until morning."

"He has one more day in the dungeon," Tania added. "I mean, his job." They looked at each other and laughed.

Janie shook her head. "I thought you guys were waiting until the wedding night."

"We are," Tania confirmed. "For the full canoodle. That doesn't mean we can't do other things. It's hard being away from each other when you're used to getting some several times a week, you know?"

Keon blinked.

"But enough about our sex life," Trey said.

"How are *your* sex lives?" Tania fell onto her fiancé's lap, chortling.

Janie's eyes popped. "This call is over!" Grabbing the phone off the coffee table, she punched the red circle. "If they try again, don't answer." She chucked the phone into the bowl. The device clattered against hers.

Keon shook his head. "She didn't say where to pick up the golf shirts."

"I doubt this is about golf," Janie muttered. She crossed her arms beneath her breasts, which had the distracting effect of plumping up her cleavage in her V-necked top. "I predict she'll text me the name of the store in three, two—" In the bowl, her phone blared the wedding march. She checked the device. "There we have it. Store name, address, and phone number." She tossed the phone into the bowl.

"What's this about then? Is Tania meddling?" In his and Janie's relationship? "She doesn't seem the type."

Janie harrumphed. "She's not. I am."

Chuckling, he rubbed her upper arm. "Is she paying you back?" If that were true, he couldn't say he minded.

"I don't know. Maybe. I'm responsible for Derek and Lacey getting together two weeks ago. And...I might have played a part in introducing Tania and Trey."

That didn't seem like a screaming-banshee problem. "I don't hear anyone complaining."

A troubled expression passed over her features.

"Some people say I meddle. But I'm not a buttinsky, Keon. I just assist my friends in the romance department from time to time."

He smiled. Both his brothers could benefit from a kindhearted sister-in-law who moved heaven and earth to help them find true love.

"And now you think Tania might have meddled back? With us?"

"No. I mean, how could Tania arrange Heath's employee fracturing a wrist so he couldn't help with my wedding tasks? If not for that accident, you would run errands for Trey, and Heath would be here. With me."

"I don't know about that." All along, Keon had intended to devise a way for him and Janie to spend time together. Heath needing to step away had helped progress his mission, but he wouldn't have flown to Rosevale days early to rock back and forth on his heels, hands in the pockets of his shorts, whistling summer songs, and admiring Janie from afar until he flew home again.

She was it for him. There was no longer any doubt about it. He yearned to continue their relationship. He ached for them to be in the same place. The same country.

Not for a couple of more weeks.

For life.

Chapter Eleven

Hours later, now that she and Keon were alone—really alone—in her own apartment, Teacup having settled back in with Heath, a finger of unease slithered up Janie's spine. Battling the disagreeable sensation, she slid two individual-sized take-and-bake lasagnas into the oven, then rearranged the vase of cornflowers on her dinette table.

At the counter, the source of her restlessness emptied bagged salad into a big wooden bowl. Heart beating rapidly, Janie drank in the sight of Keon's striking black brows, full lips, and the sexy stubble darkening his jaw. During last spring and summer, they'd prepared dozens of meals together at her place, most cooked from scratch. He knew where she kept her dishes and flatware. Her kitchen towels. Her bathroom towels. Her sheets and pillowcases. Even her bras and underwear. So then why did she feel antsy?

She *wanted* to focus on their relationship without wedding tasks or a hyperactive dog interfering. They desperately needed this couple time.

Except...were they a couple again? She chewed her lower lip. For how long? The question had haunted her since this afternoon's embarrassing video-chat with Tania and Trey.

If only the bride hadn't brought up Janie's sex life. Or lack of one. Or Keon's sex life, which did not lack, considering his revelations about two of his exes.

And Janie hadn't needed to hear about Tania and Trey's plans for entertaining themselves until morning!

Earlier, Keon said he didn't want to pressure her about sex. His thoughtfulness should flood her with relief. Shouldn't it?

Janie didn't consider herself much of a seductress. To her way of thinking, the best acts of making love occurred naturally. Like the night of the outdoor concert when Keon lived in Washington.

And every night they'd slept together last June and July.

But if she didn't make a move on him tonight, if *he* didn't drag her into his sex-god cave, did that spell trouble for their future relationship? Would he forget her again, eventually, after he flew home?

Yes, she was obsessing, but she couldn't seem to stop. Like an unbridled mare, her fears had clippity-clopped into the deepest gully of worrywart hell. The solution seemed obvious. She needed to *propel* them over this hurdle. Then she would have clarity.

Nerves prickling, she strolled into the kitchen in bare feet. She let her shoulder brush his as she reached for plates in the cupboard above her favorite grouping of African violets. He opened the refrigerator.

"Looking for something?" she asked huskily, setting the plates on the counter. Her gaze lingered on his firm behind in the navy shorts that ended right above his knees.

Head lowered, he moved around items in her fridge. "Yeah." Jars and cartons jostled on the shelves, and his deep voice echoed off the interior of the appliance. "Do you want red wine or white wine with the lasagna?" he asked without turning.

She smiled. "Who keeps red wine in the fridge?"

"I've taken to it after opening a bottle. Refrigerating some reds slows oxidization."

"Say what?"

"The chemical reaction once the wine is exposed to oxygen," Keon clarified, head remaining buried, but his delectable butt displayed to perfection.

"Well, you learn something new every day," Janie purred, snaking down a hand and pinching his butt. Her fingertips skidded on solid muscle, and he swore as his skull clunked the underside of her top freezer door.

Straightening, he rubbed his head, a bottle of white wine clutched in his other hand.

Her face burned. "Sorry. It looked like it needed pinching."

He laughed. "No problem." The fridge door swung shut. "Maybe next time, not when my head is in the fridge. Or I'm standing on a ladder. About to rappel down a cliff. That sort of thing." He put down the bottle, wrapped her in his arms, and placed a sensuous kiss on her mouth.

Janie sighed, loving their physical connection despite her abysmal seduction tactics.

"How long do these lasagnas take?" he asked, fingers threading through her hair.

Closing her eyes, she moaned. "Twenty-five minutes."

He nuzzled her neck, and sensuous goosebumps dotted her skin.

"That's not long enough for what I have in mind," he growled.

Their mouths joined, and her limbs weakened. It seemed Keon intended to take things to a bed. If she had anything to say about it, tonight. Tomorrow now looked iffy. Her brother had arranged a family dinner for their parents to meet Lacey, and Janie had promised to attend. She couldn't be happier for Derek and her friend. But didn't she also deserve happiness, even if only for tonight, in Keon's arms?

She drew back within his embrace, breathing heavily. "We can be quick now," she whispered. "And then, later on, take our time."

His penetrating brown gaze released sparks of arousal low in her belly. "You've got me, Janie, with or without taking this to a bed."

"How about if we take it to the sofa?" She slid her hands down his arms and entwined them with his larger ones. "I need an appetizer." But her declaration was about more than satisfying the desire for a quickie. She loved this man. She yearned to connect with him in the most intimate way possible.

"A valid argument," he responded in a solemn tone. "While I have fond memories of your couch," —he scooped his arms beneath her thighs and swung her up—"I say to the bed."

"To the bed!" Janie cheered as he carried her into her room, like he had countless times before. The soles of his feet padded on the worn hardwood. "I hope you came prepared," she hinted, switching on the lights from the shelter of his arms. She wanted to see him. Every. Spectacular. Inch. "I'm not on anything."

"You mean did I bring protection?" He shook his head. "That would be cocky."

"Uh-huh," she drawled.

"Never fear." He dumped her unceremoniously onto the mattress and opened the nightstand drawer. "If I recall, when I left, we were stocked up." He retrieved a box and extracted a packet. "Here we go. I knew I could count on you, Janie."

Climbing off the bed, she folded back her floral summer-weight duvet. "Check the expiration date."

He peered at the numbers stamped on the box. "They're okay." He tore open the packet and placed a condom on the nightstand before facing her with a devastatingly sexy smile.

Heart pounding, she reached for the hem of his

T-shirt and helped him tug it off. He returned the favor with her crop top, his hands warm on her skin.

They each shucked off their shorts and panties, and he stood before her in his full Canadian glory, which she admired with a frank stare.

"Janie," he whispered, drawing her attention upward. "You're stunning." His heated gaze drilled over her body. He tugged her back into his arms. Their mouths melded and their tongues thrusted as he unhooked her bra.

With the last barrier between their skins shed, she glided her hands over his chest. "Oh, Keon. I've missed you."

"Same," he whispered, walking her backward to the mattress.

Her spine hit the cool sheets. He fit his body over hers, and they kissed and caressed for several long minutes, her hands around his neck, on his rear, her fingers stroking his rock-hard length as his touch spiraled sensations on her breasts and nipples, her thighs and center, where his fingers found her slick and ready.

He began a slow slide down her body, kissing her breasts and tummy. She knew where he was headed—his tongue and lips doing delicious things between her legs—and she loved the idea, she craved the idea, but this time, the first time in so long, the first lovemaking of their new relationship, she needed him—

"Inside me," she said out loud. "Keon..." She moaned.

"One second." He sheathed himself with the condom. Balancing on his forearms over her body, he gazed at her with those beautiful dark brown eyes she loved, and desire stirred to a restless pitch inside her. "I feel like I've waited a lifetime to do this with you again," he whispered, positioning himself.

Her throat thickened and ached. "Same."

The tip of his erection slid into her, and she gasped. He withdrew and pushed in further. Her inner walls softened as she took him deep inside. He swept a hand beneath her rear, and she wrapped her legs around his hips, pulling him close.

Their mouths met as their bodies moved, and his lips didn't leave hers again until she neared the precipice.

As her breath came in short pants, he whispered, "Are you close?"

"I—I—" She couldn't speak for the emotion overwhelming her. She just nodded.

His hands cradled her face, his fingers at her

temples. "I love you, Janie," he whispered, placing a gentle kiss on her mouth.

Tears sprang to her eyes. "I love you too," she whispered back.

"I mean it," he said, voice low and seductive, heated, and so very cherished. "I've never said those words to another woman. I love *you*, Janie."

She cried out. "I love you. I do. I do. I love you, Keon."

He groaned. His mouth crushed hers, and her heart and body soared as she raced toward ecstasy.

Within moments, he joined her, whispering her name and his love again and again as her heart thundered and her mind spun with the sweetest bliss.

After visiting the bathroom and checking the lasagnas, Keon cuddled Janie in the double bed, his head resting on the pillow he'd thought of as his during their previous relationship and the light duvet he'd helped her choose covering their bodies. They both remained naked, and her cheek cozied against his chest as a clump of sandy-blond hair tickled his nose. He smoothed the bump and kissed the skin at her hairline. Her satisfied murmurings lifted to his ears.

"How are you?" he half-whispered, brushing back another hair lump. He'd left the bedroom door open, and the delicious scent of Italian spices wafted in.

"Never better," she responded, her warm lips curling against his skin.

"I didn't scare you off?" He might as well put his concerns front and center. He hadn't intended to strip his soul bare in the moment's passion, but a man didn't take back the words, "I love you." Nor did he want to. He had meant them. With every-thing in him.

She looked up. "I'm not sure how we're going to make this work," she said in a tender voice, lips trembling. "But I do love you, Keon Rivers. My cuddly Canadian cutie, named for a hockey player."

A grin stretched across his face. She was forever ribbing him about his 'Canadianisms,' as she termed phrases and pastimes he considered commonplace. "Yeah," he said. "My dad named me Keon after one of the greatest centers of the Toronto Maple Leafs, thereby making *me* a national treasure, and don't you forget it."

"If I haven't forgotten that charming factoid by now, I doubt I ever will."

He skimmed his palm over her shoulder to the small of her back, beneath the quilt. He and Janie were perfect together, but the logistics of their relationship remained. Without discussing options, how could they plan a future?

"You know," he began, rubbing his hand along her spine, the pad of his thumb tracing every beautiful vertebra. "I really enjoyed my year in Washington."

"I loved your year in Washington." She kissed his neck, and his lower body stirred. "But we wasted time. We could have been together all those months." She lifted her face and pressed her lips to his mouth.

He returned her kiss for kiss. "I don't know what we were thinking."

"That it's complicated?"

He nodded. "I want to be with you, Janie." His heartbeat echoed in his ears. "Maybe I should move back."

A full second elapsed. She blinked. "To Washington?" Surprise reflected in her eyes and on her face.

He nodded again.

Her forehead knitted. "Keon?" She scooted back

on the mattress and propped an elbow on the sheets. The duvet slid down her arm. "What would you do?"

He sat up, his spine against the headboard and his legs extending beneath the quilt. "Trey is still with Whitaker Organic Farms—"

"Only for the transition to that California corporation." A frown pulled at the corners of Janie's thoroughly kissed lips. "Without his dad in charge, he isn't enjoying his time there. He only agreed to stay on—for, what was it, a year or two?—to facilitate the sale."

"I realize that." The majority shareholders of the senior members of the Whitaker family voted to sell the multigenerational company to a major conglomerate last fall. "That's business." Whether or not Trey liked it. Keon's friend's wishes hadn't factored into the decision. "But he might be able to get me in again."

Janie shook her head. "And you would want that?"

"I want to be with you." Leaning over, Keon kissed her.

"I want the same thing." She inhaled. "This is—" She stopped. Started again. "It's a lot."

"We need to talk about it sometime." He caressed her shoulder.

She sat cross-legged on the mattress, the duvet covering one knee. Not the least self-conscious in her nudity, she took his hand. "I thought we might start with something more low-key."

"Such as?"

"The other day, you mentioned sticking around until Tania and Trey return from honeymoon."

"To look after Teacup? You said no." In fact, she had flat-out nixed the idea.

A pink hue colored her face. "I was hasty."

Air whistled in through his teeth. "Do you want me to stay?" His voice sounded tight. "Just so we're clear, for two weeks?"

"Yes," she responded, her fingers twitching within his.

"And after that?"

"Keon." Her gaze pleaded with him. As if he were being unreasonable. Or unrealistic. Not understanding what was at stake. Too optimistic. "Even if you stayed those two weeks, don't you need to plan with your family first? With your mom and dad? About your role at the garden center?"

"Yes. It's short notice, but I'm happy to call them."

Long hair flowing around her shoulders, Janie shook her head again. Her right-before-a-rain eyes narrowed like a bootylicious TV detective's solving a mystery. "If it's *short notice* to arrange two more weeks off during Hamaguchi's busiest season, why bring it up?"

He paused, sensing a female-logic trap on the horizon. "Strictly speaking, May and June are busy too. And you brought up the additional weeks. A second ago."

The color on her cheeks deepened. "*You* brought it up. *Yesterday*."

"It seemed like a good idea at the time."

"At the time?"

"As a way to ease you into things."

"To ease me *into* things?" Sparks of irritation flared in her eyes.

Why was she parroting everything he said? He squeezed her hand. "Janie, I love you. I love you now, and I loved you yesterday. I loved you the day before that, and I loved you when I stepped off the plane on Sunday. The truth is, I fell in love with you last summer. Because I'm an idiot, it took a few months to sink in."

"And I love you. I was just as much an idiot last summer as you were."

That settled it. They were both idiots. "Then the issue is?"

Her voice softened. "Keon, I can't ask you to give up everything you and your family have planned since you were a child. To move here. For me."

"Why not?" People changed their lives for love every day.

"Because," she stated simply, "it's *your* life. You like it the way it is."

"I would *love* it with you in it."

Her chin firmed. "You were raised to run Hamaguchi's—"

"And now my lazy-ass brothers can run it instead. Problem solved."

"Oh, no, you don't." She flung away his hand and climbed off the bed. Not bothering with her bra and panties, she yanked on her shorts and top.

Tossing back the quilt, he reached for his boxers and shorts. "No, I don't what?" He zipped up.

"Get to decide to sacrifice your dreams for me."

"Janie." Dragging on his T-shirt, he went to her side of the bed. "I have options. *We* have options. I can try to get in with Whitaker Organic Farms again. I can ask Trey if he wants a partner in his startup once he's at that point."

"And I'm saying those choices are too big—no,

too huge, too massively large-scale—for you to make on a whim."

"This isn't a whim," he insisted, his voice gruffer and louder than he'd intended. "I came here early to find out if we have a future."

She crossed her arms. "I thought you came to help with wedding stuff."

"*And* to figure us out."

Her hands spread. "Well, I don't know if I'm there yet."

"Not there yet?" Now he was parroting her. "What the hell?"

"Keon. We went from extending your visit to upending your life." She snapped her fingers. "Quick as that. From two more weeks in Rosevale to casting off a business built by your grandparents from the literal ground up."

"I take it back. My brothers aren't lazy asses. They can handle Hamaguchi's. I might have to fly home now and again—"

"But you're the oldest. And you want it."

Yes, he wanted it. He had always wanted it. "I want you more."

"Your family needs you."

"Is this your way of saying you don't?"

Her eyes tapered to slits in frustration. "I will

not," she enunciated, "allow you to give up your family's goals and dreams for me. I will not do it, Keon."

He lifted his hands. Moments ago, she'd said she loved him. But only for short bursts? For a summer visit and perhaps a few months following?

Not the lifetime he'd envisioned. Not the inter-lacing of *their* goals. *Their* dreams.

What kind of love was that?

Chapter Twelve

THE STOVE TIMER blasted from the kitchen. "The lasagnas," Janie muttered, jabbing a finger at this infuriating, frustrating man she loved, "are done." She stomped out of the bedroom.

In a flash, he overtook her, walking backward in bare feet, gaze steady on her face as she beelined for the stove. "The lasagnas can wait."

She stuck out her chin. "They'll burn."

"I don't give a shiny shoelace."

"I do." Pushing past him, she grabbed two potholders, flung open the oven door, and whipped out the hot containers, steam searing her chin. She thumped the sizzling meals onto the range.

"Janie."

The weight of his gaze tracked her movements as she rolled open the flatware drawer and snatched fistfuls of forks and knives. She couldn't blame him if he was confused. *She* was confused. What had made him think she would agree to sacrificing every aspect of his life? It wasn't a matter of short-term or long-term. It was more complex. There was no getting around the fact that moving to Washington carried a heightened risk for Keon that the business and home and family waiting for him back in BC did not.

Keon Rivers was the most sensible, settled, rational person she knew. Since the day they'd met, he'd described his life as a fulfilling straight line stretching out in front of him. Family. Business. Roots. Tradition.

And now he wanted to throw it away. For her?

How *dare* he? Except...what did she expect him to do? If he didn't move back to Washington, what was the alternative? That she would move across the border? Her heart pounded. The idea both excited and terrified her. Why wasn't he terrified?

Stiff fingers splaying, she let the flatware fall onto the plates as if she were executing a mic-drop. She clutched the potholders and transferred each lasagna to a plate. Knocked a fork onto the counter and returned it to its spot. Carried the meals to the table and plunked them onto her irritatingly cheerful blue-and-yellow placemats, cutlery clinking.

Turning, she asked, "Why didn't you ask *me* to move to Canada?"

He shook his head, eyes wide. "You've never been outside the US. I lived here a year."

"Oh, so because I haven't traveled farther than a California theme park, I can't envision us being together unless we agree on my home country? What about *your* home country?"

"Where is this coming from? Janie, if you want to move to Canada, I'll support you all the way."

She pointed at him. "Ah-ha!" She marched into the kitchen, grabbed the salad, and, delicately this time, placed the bowl on the table.

Keon pressed his fingertips to his forehead. "I don't understand what's happening."

That made both of them. "Then I'll clarify." She collected individual salad bowls and his favorite dressing. "You don't *want* to move to the States." She delivered the items to the table. "Your year away from home was for a specific purpose. And before you say you did more than work for Whitaker Organic Farms during your time in the US, allow me to summarize." She counted off the highlights on her fingers. "You came to hang out with your long-time buddies, Trey and Heath. *Yes.* To visit Vegas, the Grand Canyon, and the other jaunts on your American bucket list. *Yes.* To take that university extension course that wasn't offered in BC. *Yes.* But also—and this is the biggie—to learn as much as possible from Whitaker Organic Farms and take that knowledge back to your family for the Hamaguchi's expansion, which is only now getting under way. Keon, while you were here, you never, ever, ever, ever"—she punctuated each *ever* with a stab of her finger—"mentioned the possibility, or the slightest desire, or an inkling of an idea, to relocate. You're only suggesting it now—"

"Because I love you," he shouted, arms flinging wide.

His sweet words couldn't sway her. She was on a roll. "Doesn't Canada have Green cards?"

"PR cards. Permanent Resident cards. Some people call them Maple Leaf cards."

She planted her hands on her hips. "*Well?*"

He stepped toward her, palms open in a let's be-reasonable manner women around the world would crumple into an imaginary paper ball and toss in the trash, if they could. "Either of us can emigrate. Geography isn't a stopper."

Tears stung her eyes. "You're assuming our relationship will be a roaring success. But what if we keep going and..." A dark hole gaped open inside her. Like autumn leaves caught in a cold gust of wind, her feistiness swirled into wings of nothingness and flitted away. "And it's not?" she whispered, sorrow pressing heavily on her shoulders.

"Oh, Janie." He wrapped her in one of his infamous bear hugs.

She sniffled against his T-shirt. "I've seen how difficult negotiating a change in extended-family dynamics was for Trey. I don't want that for you. Your grandparents gave up everything to move to Canada—"

"And begin the adventure of a lifetime." He dropped a soft kiss to her forehead. "They don't regret it." His gaze found hers.

"It couldn't have been easy." Her voice squeaked.

"What good thing is? But they made it work and look where they are now. They created a thriving business that they passed on to their daughter and son-in-law, and they look back on those years with pride. My parents worked alongside them. They have three devoted grandsons." He paused. "Okay, they have me and two so-so grandsons."

Janie gave a watery smile. "You love your brothers. Plus, you're arguing my points."

"Let's turn this around. What would you give up if you moved? A twin brother—"

"He's younger than me by four minutes. And I've decided he's a so-so sibling, like yours."

Keon smiled. "You love him to death. You also have great parents and a wonderful network of friends who are now my friends. You've never met my BC friends."

"But I could."

"Yes." He kissed her cheek. "Janie, you've worked for Sunshine & Roses since you were in high school. The Murdochs paid for your floral-design and business courses. You're set to become manager, maybe even buy them out someday."

She wiped a hand across her nose. "Manager, yes. Roslyn hasn't mentioned selling."

"It could happen."

"*You're* opening a flower shop—"

"Which I would love to be yours."

Air swept into her lungs. Were they discussing the possibility of her running Hamaguchi's floral department? "I would call it Janie's Blossoms," she whispered.

His lips tilted in a sexy grin. "That's cute. My mom and obaasan would love it."

"Would they?" Janie had yet to meet his mom or grandmother. She hadn't spoken to any of his BC friends or relatives in a video-chat or phone call. Until this point, they'd been ultra-careful about not inviting questions or raising expectations outside their Rosevale friend group.

Despite the love burgeoning inside her, she couldn't ignore the hazards of agreeing to move forward with him right now. Worries ate at her. Like, what if she uprooted herself to move to the Okanagan Valley and then his family didn't like her? Or, for whatever reason, their relationship didn't work out?

She would wind up hurt far worse than she'd been last year.

Tears dampened her lashes. She whispered, "We each need to take a step back and consider what's at stake."

A slow sigh seeped from his lips. "You said it in your bedroom. Emotionally, we aren't on the same page." His tone didn't hold a sliver of accusation.

"We love each other, but we're stuck in different countries."

Even as her heart splintered into fragments, Janie grappled for reason. "When you left, it tore me up," she said. "I can't bear to go through that again." She would become a walking wound.

"Don't be afraid," he murmured, brushing gentle knuckles across her cheek. "I want a life with you. I can't guarantee everything will come up sunshine and roses, but I predict overflowing baskets of Janie's blossoms."

His corniness touched her heart. "Can we talk about this tomorrow?"

"While hauling in plants from Trey's and picking up sunroom furniture? That doesn't sound very romantic. You have a family dinner, and Friday through Sunday is booked solid with wedding events. If we don't have this conversation now, when will we?"

Her shoulders sagged. "I don't know."

His gaze clouded. "Okay then." He stepped back, his hands sliding down her arms and drifting from her wrists to her hands and fingertips. He relinquished the connection completely. "I'll make this easy on you, which, ironically, was what I was trying to do by suggesting I move back."

She bristled at his sharp tone. "Yes, suggesting *you* relocate and then holding it against me when we hit a bump, as all relationships do."

He tossed her a stone-cold look. "Nice generalization. I'm not like that, and you know it." He strode to the foyer.

Stomach sinking, she followed.

"Can I have the keys to the condo?" He raked a hand through his jet-black hair and stuffed his feet into his sandals.

"What for?"

"Like you said, we both have a lot of thinking to do. I have Heath's truck. I'll pick up the sunroom furniture and move over Tania's plants on my own." He retrieved the bag carrying the *Last Chance for Bromance* golf shirts from the foyer bench he had helped her choose during their weekend trip to Poulsbo. He jostled the bag. "I'll deliver these to the guys at the golf course on Friday."

Janie folded her arms across her middle. "What about Teacup?"

"Heath and his clerk can handle her in the back of the skate shop for one day."

Silently, Janie dug the condo keys out of her purse and handed them over.

"See you at the rehearsal dinner." Keon reached for the door.

Her heart ached. "Not before?"

"What's the point? I'm not staying for two more weeks. I'm not moving. I'm attending this wedding, and then I'm flying home. Where, as you keep reminding me, I belong."

Chapter Thirteen

CLENCHING THE VIDEO-GAME CONTROLLER, Keon punched and zapped his character's way across the colorful fantasy landscape glowing from Heath's TV. Teacup nuzzled on a blanket between his thigh and the armrest, ears pricking as their host moved noisily around in his bedroom, preparing for an evening out.

After another minute, Heath strolled into the living room, buttoning his shirt. His gaze wandered to Keon hunched on the couch. Heath picked up the remote and lowered the volume.

"Hey, numb nuts. You still here?"

"As if you didn't know," Keon responded in a monotone, jabbing a button. He couldn't muster the energy to engage in Heath's jovial brand of verbal sparring. "Where else would I be?" Not with Janie, that was for sure. After his jackass comments yesterday, would she spare him a glance during the wedding rehearsal? His stomach soured as he recalled his thoughtless statements.

"I'm not staying."

"I'm not moving."

"What's the point?"

He had bailed at the first sign of trouble. Way to go toward alleviating her perfectly reasonable concerns.

Until Keon had cemented his lonely future with the stupidest comments any man on either side of the border had spewed over the last two or three hundred years, he had visualized he and Janie exchanging knowing glances during the rehearsal dinner, the news of their reunion secret for a few days, so as not to steal the thunder from the bride and groom.

But now he would be lucky if, at the reception Saturday, she joined the tail of a Congo line he headed. Or *didn't* skedaddle out of the banquet room when Tania tossed the bouquet.

"The wedding hotel," Heath said, knocking on

Keon's skull. "Hey. Numb. Nuts. Isn't check-in at three?"

Keon craned his neck around his friend to the TV. Damn it, his character had missed a prime opportunity to throw a weapon. "Why, Heap? Am I cramping your style?" Keon had assumed Heath would stay at the skate shop until five, providing him plenty of opportunity to brood.

"Not saying you are and not saying you aren't." Heath smoothed his crisp white dress shirt over new-looking jeans. "But dude. You're in a mood."

"Yeah, yeah." Keon hadn't needed to spell out that he had royally messed up with Janie. Heath had reached the rather obvious conclusion three minutes after he'd walked through the door.

Heath sank onto the couch, grabbed a controller, and joined the massive-multiplayer game. Fingers rapid on the controls, he maneuvered his character into achieving the same moves at which Keon sucked.

"Seems a shame you're wallowing in self-pity instead of romancing Janie away from a boring family dinner," Heath commented as their characters joined forces to battle a buff fantasy villain.

"She doesn't want to see me."

"And you know that? How?"

"Because *I* wouldn't want anything to do with my sorry ass after the way I acted."

Heath snorted. "That's some piss-poor Canadian logic."

Teacup roused beside Keon, shaking off sleep. The dog bounded across his lap and landed on Heath's soft parts.

Moaning, Heath nudged the animal. "Teacup. I love ya, girl, but those are my jewels."

"Smart dog thinks you shouldn't procreate," Keon joshed, the black cloud looming above his head beginning to clear.

Heath launched a winning move at their opponent. "Booyah!" Exiting the game, he clapped Keon's shoulder. "You gotta razzle her, bud."

"What does that even mean?"

"If she's not in a place to listen to how you feel, how about showing her?"

Keon eyed his three-years-younger friend. "When did you turn into a relationship whiz?"

"Around the time my brother dropped onto his knees and begged me to be his best man. It's easier to pinpoint wrinkles in other people's lives than it is to manage your own."

"Noted. Might I point out, you're single?"

"I'm a young pup. Do *you* want to be single?"

Heath scooped up Teacup. Carrying the dog football-style, he fetched treats and waste bags from the kitchen counter.

Keon frowned. "You're taking T-Dog with you? Is she your chick magnet?"

"Not saying she is and not saying she isn't." At the entry door, Heath grinned. Teacup's golden head swiveled toward Keon. Brown eyes bright, the dog barked as they left.

Feeling more alone than he had in a year, Keon tossed down his controller. The clattering of the device on the coffee table echoed in the empty space.

Fingernails scraping his scalp, he dragged both hands through his hair and sagged against the couch cushions.

No, he did *not* want to be single.

He had told Janie he wanted a lifetime. Once they'd factored in the tricky-to-untangle ties to his family's business, she had shied away from an on-the-spot commitment.

She must have considered the idea in some small capacity, or she wouldn't have brought up naming the garden center's flower shop Janie's Blossoms.

Excitement built within him. He bent forward, hands on his knees.

A plan percolated.

He jumped off the couch.

Janie wriggled her fork into her mom's wonderful-smelling buttered herbed rice but didn't succeed in much more than shifting around the grains on her plate. Everyone else at the dining table—Mom and Dad, Derek and Lacey—engaged in lively conversation, but Janie didn't have the stomach for it, ironic pun and all.

Mom's forehead furrowed. "Honey, you're not eating," she said in a pleasant voice.

"As in, she's not scarfing down your delicious cooking for once?" Derek sent Janie a glance across the table.

"She does not scarf," Mom defended. She looked at Lacey, seated to Derek's left. "She really doesn't."

Lacey's blue eyes twinkled. "I've seen her scarf down Alicia's cupcakes a time or two."

Derek chuckled and tucked his girlfriend's hand into his on the tablecloth. The couple exchanged a besotted look.

Janie curled her upper lip at her twin. "Hardy-har." Trying not to be a party-pooper and failing miserably, she skewered a portion of rosemary roasted chicken and lifted her fork to her mouth. She chewed the tasty poultry and forced herself to swallow. She wished she could forget last night's setback with Keon and celebrate Lacey and Derek's flourishing romance and Lacey's achievement of procuring funding for her fledgling lingerie design company, but regret lodged in her veins like hardened glue, miring her thoughts.

Last night at her apartment, she had screwed up big time. Enough that Keon had avoided spending one minute in her pessimistic company today. Or even communicating with her.

For example, this morning she'd sent a text asking if he was okay, and he hadn't answered. She knew from Tania that a last-minute mix-up had occurred with the sunroom furniture, requiring Keon to drive into Seattle. But if he could answer frantic messages from the bride, couldn't he have tossed Janie a couple of growly-faced emoticons?

In return, she would have poured out her misery, begging his forgiveness and announcing she was ready to pack up her life and haul her suitcases across the border.

Her heart tattooed at a rapid pace beneath her breastbone.

She shouldn't make promises she couldn't keep.

But—but—why couldn't she keep them?

What, exactly, other than a major case of the butterflies and an aversion to white vinegar on French fries, stood in her way?

Her ears buzzed. She glanced up from selecting another chunk of chicken. Four sets of eyes scrutinized her.

Her father lifted his butter knife. "Don't ignore your mother, Janie Jumping Bean."

"I'm sorry." She flattened her palms on the tablecloth. "Did you say something?" she asked her mom.

"Yes. There's something wrong. I can tell, honey. We're family. Spill the tea. Or the beans. Or whatever it is the kids are calling it these days."

"Tea is gossip," Lacey said. "Beans are more like a secret that slips out."

Mom spread her hands. "Well, then, she can just spill her guts." She looked at Janie. "That still means telling your worried mother what's going on, doesn't it?"

Heat crawled up Janie's neck. "I don't know where to begin."

"She's in the dumps about Keon," Derek said.

Janie scoffed. "How would you know?"

"Now, now." Mom's tone held a warning.

Lacey's eyes widened. "The girls have been keeping tabs."

Janie gasped, a sob rising in her throat. "Does everyone know my business?" She sounded like a whiny child on the verge of ruining Lacey's introduction to the McAllister clan because of the frustration stemming from *her* romantic failures. Last summer, if she'd bothered to introduce Keon to her parents as more than a guy she was casually dating inside their group of friends, he might sit beside her tonight, part of her life in at least a semi-permanent fashion.

Both her parents liked and approved of Keon. A few days after he flew home, her mom mentioned how well he and Janie got along, how handsome he was, how considerate and hardworking. And polite.

It was Janie who, over the subsequent weeks, had insisted an expiration date stamped their relationship—like the package of condoms in her nightstand, which was kind of insulting now that she thought about it.

Then she'd ghosted him, emphasizing her point.

One of Derek's shoulders lifted in a shrug. "Probably, yeah, most of your women friends and I'd say a good portion of the guys know the ins and outs of what is and isn't going on between you and Keon. You can't be upset about that...big sis, considering your track record helping other couples get together. Including us." He motioned to Lacey.

"I agree," Lacey chimed. "Thank you for meddling so thoroughly in Derek's love life. You're a wonderful sister and a great friend."

Mom placed a hand on her chest, addressing Lacey. "I'm thrilled to bits you and Derek found each other."

Dad slid his glasses down his nose and stared Janie dead in the eyes. "Time for *you* to find someone."

"She has," Derek pronounced.

Janie's cheeks sizzled like eggs frying in a pan. Her marginally younger brother annoyed her to no end sometimes, no matter how much she loved him. If only she hadn't stuck her nose into *his* business less than two weeks ago, she would haul him into his old bedroom right now and light a fire beneath his butt with the Bunsen burner from his middle-school science kit.

"Honey," Mom said, patting Janie's hand. "It's not like we live in Texas or New York. I googled, and BC's Okanagan Valley is only five hundred miles and one pesky border crossing away. Yes, it's an international border, but we wouldn't mind if you chased after Keon and became an honorary Canadian. As long as you're happy."

"We'd visit," Dad said, nodding at Mom and Janie. "I checked your mother's search results. Wine tours, lakes for miles, and golf courses? Sign me up. If we fly, we wouldn't even need to connect through Vancouver."

"It's a minor annoyance going through Customs," Mom continued in a mild tone. "But we have passports."

Janie drew in a breath. "Every one of you is right." She looked at her family members and then at Lacey. She would miss them. But it was Keon she loved from the depths of her being. Keon she needed in her life every day. Keon she wanted to kiss goodnight as the moon climbed in the starry, ink-blue sky. "I need to do something majorly romantic to win him back."

"That's simple," Derek said, extracting his vibrating phone from a pants pocket. He glanced at the screen. "You're a talented florist. Design a bouquet at Sunshine & Roses and deliver it to his hotel room in person. On bended knee." He scraped back his chair.

Mom shook a finger at Janie's twin. "No cell phones at the dinner table."

Lacey squirmed on her chair. "Oh, oh," she said, gaze ping-ponging between Derek and Janie, "if we're talking romantic, jam-pack your apartment with a *dozen* bouquets of the prettiest blossoms in the store and invite him over."

Derek pressed his phone screen against his shirt. "Mom," he said with a long-suffering look. "I'm a cop. It's necessary to take a call now and then."

"I'm in furniture sales," Dad told Lacey. "The old work excuse doesn't fly."

Derek frowned at their father. "You know I wouldn't answer if it wasn't important." He kissed the top of Lacey's head before striding out of the dining room.

Lacey released a dreamy sigh. "Isn't he the best?"

"Yes, he is," Janie agreed. Her brother was perfect for Lacey, and Keon was the only man for her.

Now to prove—to the love of her life—that *she* was a woman worth taking a chance on.

Janie's pulse beat an energetic rhythm at the base of her throat as she entered the elevator of her apartment building. She could kiss her brother and Lacey for sparking a whirlwind of ideas that would hopefully help her get through to Keon. It had been all she could do to sit through the remainder of tonight's family dinner without blabbing her intentions over her mom's strawberry shortcake. She hadn't wanted anyone to know what she was up to. Tonight was for herself and the man she loved. If he would have her.

She didn't need to stop in at Sunshine & Roses. Everything she required to pull off the ultimate personalized romantic gesture existed in her section of her building's rooftop gardens and communal potting shed. She just needed to fetch her gloves and a variety of clay pots.

Oh, and—the thumping in her chest gathered speed as she pushed the button and the elevator car clunked before lumbering upward—the vintage wicker picnic basket from the top shelf of her hall closet would hold the prettiest transplanted annuals. The basket couldn't hold every plant but was perfect for carrying a selection to the wedding hotel.

Last summer, in a pique of heartbreak, she'd weed-whacked the blossoms she and Keon had planted. Now, she would demonstrate, in the best way she knew, that not only she but every plant she owned were willing to uproot themselves and move to Canada.

Alone in the elevator she stared at the doors. She had no clue if transporting live plants across the border was permitted. That wasn't the point. Moments ago, she'd messaged Heath to confirm Keon had moved to the wedding hotel. Teacup was out with Heath doing something fun, but apparently the dog was moping, suffering Keon's absence.

Janie empathized. Except, she was *done* moping. Finished placing limits on her hopes and dreams. If Keon turned her away, unimpressed, she would slink home and condemn herself to a lonely night of replanting. But then tomorrow she would drag herself out of bed, ignoring the purple bags beneath her red-streaked eyes betraying her exhaustion, and find another way to show him they were meant to be together. Even if that meant missing the bridesmaids' spa day or the wedding rehearsal to accomplish her goal.

The elevator chimed and the doors opened. Hands shaking, Janie hurried down the hall. The keychain dangled from her fingers as she aimed her key at her lock. The tip struck the deadbolt, and the ring of keys fell to the carpet. Emitting a huff, she retrieved the ring...and noticed a slivery wash of amber light shining from beneath the bottom of the door.

Had she neglected to turn off a switch?

She tested the knob. Unlocked.

Double dunce! She rolled her eyes.

Opening the door, she deposited her purse and keys onto the bench in a practiced gesture. The entryway was dark, but a curious glimmer flickered from the kitchen.

She wandered deeper inside, her eyes slowly sweeping everywhere as her sluggish mind processed what was around the room.

Countless candles—squat candles, tall candles, slim candles, white candles, red candles, heart-festooned candles, even a few Canadian-maple-leaf-decorated candles—glowed in a heart-shaped arrangement on her dinette table.

Not only that, but bunches of buds and blooms in a variety of colors extended and, in some cases, flopped romantically from an array of vases. On her coffee and side tables. On the kitchen countertops.

She tugged in a breath. These weren't just any flowers—

Her next thought evaporated as Keon emerged

from the shadows near her bedroom door, a sexy smile slanting his mouth. He held out a hand-tied bouquet of brilliant red roses mixed with vibrant whites and lush greenery. "Janie..."

"Keon," she exclaimed, moved and touched and simply wowed. "You did all this? For me? For us? Oh, my God," she whispered on an inward breath. "I love you."

Chapter Fourteen

KEON'S HEART SKIPPED A BEAT. "And I love you, Janie McAllister. I don't want to go another day without you by my side."

Tears sparkled in her gray-blue eyes. "You won't have to, Keon Rivers." Her earnest tone mirrored his. She accepted the bouquet and inhaled the heady fragrance of the red and white roses. "I want to be with you. Always." She dipped her nose to the petals again. "These are lovely," she whispered, glancing up. "Thank you."

"Roslyn met me a few hours ago at Sunshine & Roses," he explained, placing an arm around Janie's shoulders. He kissed her soft, pink lips. "She talked me through choosing the stems and removing the thorns."

Janie's smile stretched across her face. "You did a fabulous job."

He couldn't help but grin in response. Did she really have no idea what was about to go down? Good thing he intended to propose only once in his life.

First, he needed to lay the groundwork. "Derek lent me a key to your place," he said as they strolled to the table. He took the bouquet and placed the arrangement in a large vase in the middle of the heart-shaped candle design.

"That was you on the phone with him earlier?" Janie asked with a hopeful look.

Nodding, he clasped her hands. "I want to show you something."

"Me first. I need to say this." Her fingers trembled against his palms. "Keon, I'm so sorry for last night." Gazing into his eyes, she inhaled a long breath. "I want to be with you and see where it leads. Just so we're clear, I'm banking on a lifetime. And...I want to run your family's flower shop, if they agree. But, baby, I plan to move to BC regardless."

Joy mushroomed in his heart. He hadn't even popped the question yet. This woman never failed to surprise him. "You want to relocate?"

Tenderness softened her gaze. "In an instant.

Keon, I love you. Your life is in Canada. Yes, I have my family and friends here, but I'll finally get to meet *your* family. Your friends. I want to jump in. To go on a grand adventure, like your grandparents did. They uprooted everything they knew in Japan to start a new life in British Columbia. My adventure is only a hop, skip, and a jump across the border, but I'm with you, baby, all the way."

He kissed her. "And if my family and friends don't like you, like you feared?" he teased.

"Ohhhh." Her gaze narrowed playfully. "They won't be able to resist me."

"You're right. Who could? Not me." Not since they'd met. He hauled her into his arms, inhaling her sunshiny scent. As they kissed and caressed, he restrained himself from allowing the moment to grow too heated. Slipping an arm around her waist, he pulled out his phone. "Speaking of my family, they put something together. Call me presumptuous, but I think you'll like it." After her comments yesterday—and also of a moment ago—he would stake the rest of his life on it.

He selected the video and pressed play.

Janie's mouth fell open as his parents appeared on the screen. His mom begged her to put her oldest son out of his misery and join Keon in Canada. His dad stood behind Mom, hands up and lips pulling in a 'don't blame me, I'm only the husband' expression.

Janie laughed.

Keon smiled as the next scenes displayed his paternal and then maternal grandparents, the latter wearing *Hamaguchi's Fruit and Garden Centre* T-shirts. His ojiisan spoke in Japanese while Baachan translated, gifting Janie the pleasure of hearing their invitation twice: "Yes, please, run Janie's Blossoms!"

She teared up. "How did they—?"

"I might have said something."

Her hand flew to her mouth. She giggled as images of his brothers and two of his friends followed. Hell, yeah, every one of them wanted Janie to move to the Okanagan, manage Hamaguchi's cut-floral division, enrich their lives, but most of all, bring back the smile to Keon's face that evidently had been missing for a year.

"Keon, this is amazing. How did you do this?"

He kissed her. "Once my mom sets her mind on something, she can't be stopped. The video was short notice, but she pulled it off." Stepping behind his love, he hugged Janie around the waist as the clip ended.

She passed back his phone, and he nuzzled her

neck as they rocked back and forth. She swept out a hand, indicating the vases. "Where did you get these gorgeous plants?"

"Your rooftop garden." He kissed the goose-bumps dotting her skin.

Her hands clasped his forearms around her waist. "Oh, no. Keon, that's not possible."

"With love, anything is possible," he said, sounding wise, if he said so himself. Brushing back a silky swathe of her hair, he rained kisses on her nape. "I hope you're not mad," he said as she squirmed and sighed. He'd taken a chance digging up these buds. "Last year, our garden succumbed to heartbreak. This year, the plants represent that our love is portable. It goes where we are, as long as we're together."

"It's kind of serendipitous," she agreed in a hushed voice. "I was planning to unearth a variety of annuals and bring them to the hotel."

"I beat you to it." He was brilliant.

Janie looked around, her gaze searching his. "Except...these flowers aren't mine."

"They"—his eyebrows hoisted—"aren't?"

She shook her head. "The weed-whacking felt like bad mojo. I wasn't going to plant anything this year, but a couple on the second floor volunteered to swap plots."

He moaned. "Oh, boy. I figured you wanted different colors. Sounds like I have some explaining to do."

She laughed. "They'll understand. We're together now. That's what counts."

He hoped her gardening buddies felt the same.

Swiveling in his arms, she placed a juicy smacker on his lips. "I love the video *and* the flowers. And the candles, especially the maple leaf ones."

His heart leaped. Clasping her left hand, he withdrew a small silver box from his pants pocket. As the candlelight played over her face, he lowered to one knee.

"And what do you say to this?" he asked around a tight throat, opening the box with his thumb. A diamond engagement ring sparkled against the red interior.

"Keon?" Her hand shook.

He removed the ring from the box without freeing her fingers. "Janie, I love and adore you. I never want you to feel like you have to weed-whack a garden because of me again in this or any lifetime. If you ever do feel that way, sweetheart, please tell me. We'll work it out. Honey, I want you to plant as many gardens as you like." He sounded corny, but he didn't care. Their first time around, he'd buried his feelings, and they'd lost precious time.

She released a heartfelt sob. "And I...I want to plant those gardens," she whispered.

He smiled. He positioned the ring at the tip of her fourth left finger. "Janie McAllister, love of my life. Will you do me the honor of making me the happiest man on the planet and marry me?"

Happy tears trickled down her cheeks. "And become an honorary Canadian?" she whispered.

"We'll need to work on your politeness to satisfy the Sorry Council, but I'd say you stand an extraordinary chance."

"Then, oh, Keon, yes, I'll marry you!"

Happiness flooding him, he slipped the ring onto her finger.

She reached down and cupped his face. Her fingertips grazed his stubble. "Oh, my gosh, get up here." Tugging Keon to his feet, she threw her arms around him. "Sorry, but can you ask me again?"

There was his honorary Canadian, slipping in the country's favorite word.

"Marry me?" he whispered.

Her lips parted. A beat passed. "Yes," she breathed.

He pumped prizefighter fists into the air. "Yes!"

Scooping her up, he carried her around the table. They took turns blowing out the candles so her apartment wouldn't burn down while they scorched the sheets.

"I love you, Janie," he whispered.

"I love you," she whispered back, head nestled on his shoulder.

Feeling more certain about anything than he ever had in his life, he carried his cherished fiancée into her bedroom and kicked the door shut.

He couldn't wait until she became his wife.

Don't miss **Trusting Trey**, the next and last book in *Love & Other Calamities!*

Trusting Trey features Tania Hoyt and Trey Whitaker, the bride and groom for the upcoming wedding (if it occurs...)

The story

The flawless wedding day Tania Hoyt dreams about crumbles to ashes when her shoes are ruined, fire destroys the church, and her deadbeat dad blows in, upending the family apple cart. After a summer of far too many mishaps and the mother of all surprises, Tania worries if the universe is trying to drop her a mega-clue that she and fiancé Trey Whitaker simply aren't meant to be.

But Trey can't lose her. He only has hours to pull together a happy ending and prove he's the man—and the husband—Tania deserves.

Acknowledgments

Thank you to Mary J. Forbes for her fabulous job of being my First Eyes on this manuscript. You can always see the forest through my literary trees.

Thanks as well to Nina Langton and Tom Ouchi for answering my questions about Japanese grandparent naming conventions.

Also, I am indebted to my grade 9 algebra teacher for unwittingly lending his name to *Hamaguchi's Fruit and Garden Centre*, spelled the Canadian way, ending in RE. From the morning Mr. Hamaguchi walked into our classroom, all serious-looking with his 1970s perm, to the time he gently chided me for writing Procter Power all over the grade 10 Student Council posters, he was one of only two high school teachers who succeeded in infiltrating my brain with anything math-like.

About the Author

Cindy Procter-King writes steamy romcoms and contemporary romances bursting with laughter and emotion. Sassy, feel-good fiction!

Cindy's books are available from eBook retailers all over the world, as well as in trade paperback, some library hardcover and large print, and some foreign editions.

Cindy lives in Canada with her family, Ghost'Da Allie McBeagle, and too many grand-dogs to count!

For more on Cindy's books, visit:
www.cindyprocter-king.com

facebook.com/cindyprocterkingauthor

instagram.com/cindyprocterking

bookbub.com/authors/cindy-procter-king

x.com/cindypk

Crave another sassy romance?

www.readsassyromance.com